THE EGG
MAN

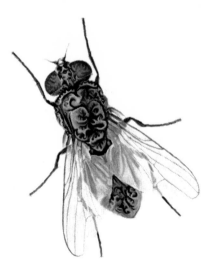

Also by CARLTON MELLICK III

Satan Burger
Electric Jesus Corpse
Sunset With a Beard (stories)
Razor Wire Pubic Hair
Teeth and Tongue Landscape
The Steel Breakfast Era
The Baby Jesus Butt Plug
Fishy-fleshed
The Menstruating Mall
Ocean of Lard (with Kevin L. Donihe)
Punk Land
Sex and Death in Television Town
Sea of the Patchwork Cats
The Haunted Vagina
Cancer-cute (Avant Punk Army Exclusive)
War Slut
Sausagey Santa
Ugly Heaven, Beautiful Hell (with Jeffrey Thomas)
Adolf in Wonderland
Ultra Fuckers
Cybernetrix

The Egg Man

CARLTON MELLICK III

AVANT PUNK

AVANT PUNK

AN IMPRINT OF ERASERHEAD PRESS

ERASERHEAD PRESS
205 NE BRYANT
PORTLAND, OR 97211

WWW.ERASERHEADPRESS.COM

ISBN: 1-933929-74-X

AUTHOR'S NOTE

Since I was 12, I always wanted to write a book called *The Egg Man*. Whenever I told somebody I was going to write a book called the Egg Man, they would say oh like that Beatles song? And I would say huh? They would say you know I am the egg man, I am the walrus. And I would say what's that? Whenever I think of the egg man, I don't think of that song. The egg man, to me, is like a boogey man. When we were kids, my sister and I used to have reoccuring nightmares about a boogeyman we called the egg man. He was a white doll-like creature with an egg-shaped head, no mouth, tiny black eyes, and spindly limbs. The egg man would creep into children's bedrooms, hide under their beds, and strangle them in their sleep.

I always wanted to write about this boogey man of my youth. In the past twenty years, I plotted three different books using The Egg Man as a title. None of them were interesting enough to write. I also used the title for a screenplay about a hitman that looked kind of like humpty dumpty. It never went anywhere.

When I decided to write a book about people with giant egg-shaped brains, that I didn't have a title for, I figured I would go with The Egg Man. It has nothing to do with the boogey man I used to lose sleep over as a kid, but there is an egg man character in it.

The Egg Man is a "what if?" story. Sci-fi is a "what if?" genre, but so is bizarro. I'm a fan of this kind of a story. I like asking: what if the world was made of meat?

What if everyone in the world committed suicide at the same time? What if we carried around our souls in little jars? One of my favorite what ifs is "What if the human race evolved in a different way?"

What if we had only one gender and reproduced asexually? What if we were all born with the ability to read each other's thoughts? What if only one in a hundred people were born with the sense of sight? What if women bit the heads off of men after mating like mantids? These are the kinds of things I love to write about. I love thinking about how these differences would effect our society. If we could read each other's thoughts how would that effect dating? How would that effect government? Would we all be forced to be honest? Would we all hate each other? In The Egg Man, I ask many what ifs, mostly focused on the way humans reproduce and the way children are raised.

I hope you enjoy The Egg Man. It is a bit darker than my usual stuff, and maybe a bit more disturbing (I am easily disturbed by smells), yet also one of my most autobiographical books to date.

- CM3

Chapter #1

The fetus fly wasn't yet dead when my steel-toed boot squished into it. The thing was lying there, half dead. It was trying to cry but its vocal cords were dried out. The sun had scorched its skin and bleached the color out of its eyes. The left side of its tiny body was being eaten by black ants.

The fetus fly must have been out of the womb for quite a few months, because it was the size of a football. Most don't even get to the size of a football. Like the majority of the young, this one wasn't meant to survive. I wasn't paying attention to where I was going when I stepped on its little infant torso, spraying red and black guts all over the pavement. Stomping on it still did not kill the tiny creature. It silently cried out, twitching its little sunburnt bald head, with ants crawling in and out of holes in the side of its face. At least I had shortened its agony by a few hours. I probably should have crushed its skull to put it out of its misery but I didn't want to track fetus goop all over my new apartment.

I didn't know much about the Henry Building. The Georges Organization just gave me an address and an apartment number: 312. It was going to be my home for the next four years, whether I liked it or not. Sometimes the GO would give its graduates a good place to stay for their post-graduate practice. More often, especially with the less prospective students, a post-grad would get the cheapest (and therefore the absolute crappiest) lodgings that they could possibly find. I wasn't a high prospect according to GO. After taking just one look at the Henry Building, I could tell that they set me up with the absolute crappiest place they could find. There was no telling what kind of scum I would be living with. The kind of scum that didn't bother to sweep their steps clean of half-dead fetus flies, I guess.

The inside of the building smelled like vinegar-ham and a nutty variety of pipe tobacco smoke. It could have been worse. Some of these buildings smell like urine and dead rats. I couldn't handle a place that smelled like urine or dead rats.

The hallways buzzed as I walked through them. The place was quiet and mostly empty. The only people I met on the way to my room were two dark-skinned women smoking in the hallway on the third floor. They were speaking *Toyotan*. They were wearing faded yellow Toyota factory uniforms and were covered in grease. Both of them were on the third day of their periods. I could smell it.

Breathing through my mouth as I passed between them, they stopped speaking and eyed me. They said something to me in Toyotan. I ignored them. Once I reached apartment 312, I looked back to see that they were coming down the hallway after me. They were pissed about something.

I said do you have a problem in the common tongue.

They didn't seem to understand common. One of them with raggy short hair spit into the air and shouted something that must have been a profanity in Toyotan. There was a lot of racism between companies. Since I'm not a child of Toyota they must not like me. I have experienced similar behavior with the children of Sony, IBM and McDonald's.

I really hate the children of McDonald's. They have a way of combining snobbery with stupidity that really gets under my skin. I'm really glad that I was brought up by the GO rather than McDonald's or Sony. I've heard that those

11

kids don't have a very good upbringing. Toyotans must have an even worse upbringing if they aren't even taught common. That's the first sign of a close-minded social network.

The apartment was small. Really small. It was in the shape of an "N" with a slanted ceiling. There was a kitchen, bedroom, living room, painting studio, bathroom, and closet, just like the GO said there would be, only all six things were crammed into a single N-shaped room. The living room was just a chair and a lamp, the bed was only big enough for a twelve year old girl, the closet was just a clothes line that went over the bed, the kitchen was the size of a small dresser, the studio was just an open space by the tiny glassless window, and the bathroom was just a toilet and a sink in the corner of the room. There wasn't even a shower or a bathtub. The whole place was probably only 150 square feet. It was tiny and cramped. No more than one person could ever live here.

I was used to crammed living. I lived in a dormitory for as long as I could remember, so I was used to only having a bed and a dresser to myself. This tiny apartment was better than I have ever had, though much worse than I expected. It would have to do.

The only problem with the apartment was the smell. It wasn't a horrible smell, but it was an irritating one. The room smelled like artificial vanilla mixed with wood polish and wet dog fur. Although the scent was annoying, it could have been worse. It could have smelled like sewage. With the toilet only five feet away from my bed it would have been horrible if there was a sewage smell issuing out of it while I slept.

I only had one duffel bag with me. It contained all of my possessions in the world. I didn't bother unpacking. I preferred having all of my things in one place at all times just in case I had to leave in a hurry. It's one of those instincts that we're all born with. Kind of like the instinct to horde food and water or the instinct to reproduce.

There were several shelves lining the walls which would prove very useful in such a small space. I was given a sufficient amount of money for purchasing food, toiletries, bedding, and art materials. The shelves were perfect for these kinds of items, but I would keep my personals in my duffel bag under the bed.

I thought this place could be riddled with thieves.

I went out and took a walk down the street to get my bearings around the neighborhood. There was a convenience store on the corner. I bought some rice wine, a sandwich, and some canned foods. Eating the sandwich and taking swigs of rice wine, I continued down the block.

It was midday and not many people were out. Everyone was at work. Most people in the city were completely corporatized and stayed at their company's barracks, so they rarely got out to wander the streets. Some of them have never left their company building, some of them never see the light of day. Most companies are self-contained societies, complete with housing, cafeterias, schools, hospitals, law enforcement, and recreational facilities. Some are like nice little resorts, some like concentration camps. I was lucky that I was raised by the GO. The GO wasn't the most luxurious organization to be brought up in, but it was comfortable and we had more freedoms than most. My life sure could have been a hell of a lot worse.

Most of the shops at street level were closed down. Those that were still in business were crap. Check-cashing shops, pawn shops, porn shops, that kind of thing. The only places in the area that were any use to me were the convenience store, a laundry mat/burger joint, a burrito stand that looked a little sketchy, and a tiny record shop that couldn't possibly get much business in this location. There wasn't an art supply store, but I wasn't expecting there to be one. I knew I'd have to take the streetcar across town to get the materials I'd need to start my practice.

There was a large man of mixed race sitting on the sidewalk, watching me as I approached. He was scraping a jagged knife against a soup can, as if trying to open it.

Hey, give me a bite of your sandwich said the man, in common tongue. He had a strong accent, but I didn't recognize it. It might have been a McDonald's dialect, or maybe a Footlocker one. By the looks of his burnt dirty sweater, I assumed he was disenfranchised.

I didn't look at him and kept walking. It's better to stay far away from the disenfranchised.

The man stood up and followed me, pointing the rusty blade and twisting it. I kept walking, pretending that I was too busy drinking my wine to hear him.

I want your sandwich and your wine said the man.

He started to pick up his pace, so I just ran. I wanted to keep cool in the new neighborhood, but my survival instinct kicked in and took over. He didn't follow.

I had strong survival instincts, especially when it

came to sensing danger and getting the hell out of danger as quickly as possible. Most people don't make it very far if they don't have a strong survival instinct, though. Luck is also important. Nobody gets very far without a decent amount of luck.

The farther away from the Henry Building I got, the more industrial the landscape became. There was a large steel mill by the river and several warehouses. The buildings out this way were black and metallic. Dark smoke billowed out of five dozen chimneys that surrounded me. The air was difficult to breathe.

I was suddenly hit with a wave of rot. It was a smell like roadkill and bread mold. The street here was littered with dozens of dead fetus flies. They were the size of my hand, so they must have been over a month old. They all had the same pale skin color and looked alike, as if they came from the same mother. The toxic air probably killed them as the swarm flew overhead. They had been dead a couple days, crusted to the sidewalks, flattened by streetcars and pedestrian feet, getting eaten by bugs and the rats.

I took a different route back to the Henry Building to avoid the disenfranchised guy with the knife. Nobody confronted me on this route, but I did pass three men in red jumpsuits beating another man in a gray jumpsuit with metal bars. The man in the gray uniform wasn't moving. He was either unconscious or dead. I picked up my pace and got out of there before any of the red jumpsuits noticed me.

The Henry Building was still reasonably quiet and empty when I arrived. Most of the residents must have still been at their companies.

There was a pregnant girl sitting outside the front of the Henry Building smoking a cigarette. She had light brown skin, a wide mouth with large gray lips, and long dark hair. She was dirty. Really dirty. Her hair was beginning to dread and her clothes looked like they hadn't been changed in weeks. She wore tight jeans and a wet tank top with sweat stains in the armpits. She didn't reek of body odor, but I couldn't really smell anything over the strong clove flavor of her cigarettes.

You don't live here she said in common as I entered the building.

I said yeah I do.

She said I don't know you.

I could see her nipples through her wet shirt. She wasn't wearing a bra.

I said I just moved in to 312.

You're not OSM she said.

No I said.

They're not supposed to let any new people in unless they're OSM she said.

She puffed her clove cigarette at me. I looked down. She was barefoot. Her ashy toes tapped languidly against the pavement, as if of their own accord. Her feet were leathery. It looked like she hadn't worn shoes in a few years. That was actually a good thing. Feet don't stink as bad if the person never wears shoes. I can't handle the smell of pungent feet.

I'm from the Georges Organization I said.

I asked if anyone else in the Henry Building was from the GO.

She screwed up her lips and blew smoke at me.

I went up to my apartment, locked myself in, and stayed there for the rest of the night. Outside my door, people yelled at each other in strange languages. Somebody blared music at the end of the hallway. I couldn't recognize the genre of music. It was pretty obnoxious because the band didn't have any guitars or vocals, but it had three drummers. It was just percussion and synthesized bass.

Some guy rammed his head against my door and I jumped out of bed. That's all he did. He just rammed his head against my door for no apparent reason. I listened at the door as his footsteps faded away. I didn't understand why anyone would feel the need to do such a thing.

After that, I couldn't sleep. I was too worried that other people might decide to ram their heads against my door while I was sleeping, or try to break the door down. So, instead of sleeping, I decided to explore the room with my nose.

In the dark, I smelled the air and tried to identify my surroundings by their scent. It's kind of a weird thing to do, but all Smells do it. We can't help ourselves. I wish I would have been a Sight or maybe a Sound, but my dominant sense had to be smell.

I sniffed about 17 different scents in the air. The dominant scent was the cigarette smoke that was coming into my room from under the door. The second most dominant smell was the sink. There were actually four different scents issuing from the sink. One was the rust of the faucet metal, one was the light sewage flavor coming out of the drain, one was a rotten odor from the scum that lined the drain, and the last was an odd black pepper smell that seemed to come from the water.

I continued smelling the room. There were four varieties of dust aroma. There was a maple syrup odor coming from the closet. There was a greasy smell hidden behind the toilet. There were a few smells coming in from the outside; two forms of pollution from the nearby factories and a burnt spaghetti sauce from the window of an above neighbor's kitchen. After a couple hours, I had figured out the origins of 16 of the 17 smells. But there was one that I couldn't figure out. It smelled like fig and raw hamburger meat. It issued from the west wall of my apartment.

After smelling the wall for several minutes, I had to turn on the light to see if there was a stain there. It could have been a strange cocktail that was thrown at the wall, or maybe the grease of a sweet and spicy Asian meal was wiped along the bricks. But, after close examination, I couldn't find anything unusual about the wall. There wasn't a sticky film anywhere.

The smell didn't seem to come from the wall itself, but from something on the other side of the wall. It must have been something extremely pungent for me to be able to smell it through brick. I wondered what the heck that smell could be, racked my brain trying to figure it out, but it remained a mystery.

I fell asleep close to dawn with the room's smells attacking my nostrils.

Chapter #2

Three hours later I awoke. I couldn't handle the smells anymore and had to do something about them. I got dressed in my usual black jeans, GO logo t-shirt, olive green trenchcoat, steel-toed boots, and smog-goggles. Then I went out to get a bunch of cleaning supplies.

Many of the other residents were leaving the Henry Building at the same time. Most of them wore gray jumpsuits with OSM written on the back in white letters. The OSMs all spoke the same language. It was the same language I had heard in the hallway during the night.

A couple of the OSMs gave me dirty looks as I passed them on the stairwell. It was natural, though. Most people didn't like anyone who wasn't a part of their company. When all they know is their company's way of life, everything else just seems confusing and scary.

I couldn't pin down the ethnicity of the OSMs. They were all the same race. It seemed to be some kind of cross between Arabic and Eskimo. They all looked alike. Not just because of their race; they all looked like they came from the same parents. They might have all come from the same womb, but that would have been impossible. That many offspring couldn't possibly survive together in the streets, let alone all get picked up by the same corporation. Unless OSM had a breeding program. That would be unlikely, though. Breeding programs are a thing of the executive class.

The convenience store only had bottom brand cleaning supplies, but that was okay. I know how to get smells out of anything, even if all I've got is a bar of soap and some elbow grease. The hairy guy behind the counter could hardly speak common, which was surprising. Speaking fluent common was the most important requirement for cashiers.

Children of the GO are only taught common. The GO likes to take down the walls that separate people. They believe that corporate languages are barriers designed to segregate people. They believe that everyone would be better off if we all spoke common.

On the way home, I ran into the pregnant woman again. She was sitting on the sidewalk without any pants on. She was crying and breathing hard. Her eyes were covered by a pair of ashy smog goggles and her sweaty white tank top was being held up by her chin.

As I passed her I said are you okay?

No she said.

I said what's wrong?

She said what the fuck do you think?

I then realized what was happening. She was about to give birth.

I said is there anything I can do?

She said I've done this dozens of times before.

I said I've never seen a birth before and want to help anyway.

She asked if I had anything to put under her ass.

She said my ass is killing me.

I said I have a package of paper towels.

She said give it a try.

Then she lifted her bare butt off of the pavement and waved me over.

I slid the 4-pack of paper towels under her and she sat down on it.

Not much better she said.

Sorry I said.

I watched her huffing and puffing for a while.

She said are you just going to stand there?

I shrugged at her.

I knelt down and held one of her hands. I didn't know what else to do.

She gave me an annoyed look, but she didn't refuse my hand. Her palm was gritty and cold. When her breathing got heavy, she squeezed my hand as tight as she could.

Once it happened, she leaned back into my arm and the sweat from her hip got onto my wrist.

She said here it comes.

Her vagina opened wide and released the babies. Hundreds, maybe thousands, of tiny fetus flies fluttered out of her. They swarmed into the air and created a small cloud. I'd never seen so many fetus flies before. I'd never seen them so tiny. They were only the size of small moths. I watched as the swarm of tiny babies spread apart and went their separate ways. Half of them wouldn't survive the night. Those that made it would double in size every day. Only a few of them, if any, would live long enough to see adulthood.

After they were all gone, the woman said leave me alone.

I left her alone.

She looked exhausted. Her head slumped to her knees. She pushed the package of paper towels out from under her. They were covered in a black goop. I thought she'd better keep them. I didn't want to know what that black afterbirth smelled like.

Upon entering the Henry Building, I looked back

at the fetus flies dissipating in the distance. I wondered what it was like when I was just a fetus fly. I wondered why I was the one to survive out of all of those that I was born with. Luck, most likely. Luck had a lot to do with it. Too many fetus flies were unlucky. They died from the cold, they got zapped by bug lights, they got trapped in spider webs, they got eaten by birds, they got splattered across car windshields. And once they grew larger they were hunted by alley cats and shot with pellet guns by the neighborhood children. They got caught in the machines on the industrial side of town and they got poisoned from drinking the water in the river.

You had to be really lucky to survive infancy.

I spent several hours cleaning every centimeter of my apartment, paying close attention to the smells. The water still smelled like black pepper so I couldn't use it to wash anything. I didn't want the whole place smelling like pepper, so I boiled the water and mixed in detergent. Then I disinfected and deodorized everything. I stripped down naked and disinfected myself with the same cleaning fluid.

After I was finished, all I smelled was lemon freshness. I could breathe deeply again. I thought I'd finally be able to sleep.

I took an afternoon nap. After a couple hours, I was woken by a smell. The lemon freshness had faded and another smell had become dominant. It was the smell of fig and raw hamburger meat.

Chapter #3

Later that night I was drunk on rice wine and there was a knock at the door. It was the girl who had given birth that morning.

Hi she said.

She let herself in.

She was still wearing the same clothes as before. She reeked of clove cigarettes with a hint of body odor and something else that was rancid. I wondered if she had taken a shower since she had given birth.

She asked if she could have some of my rice wine after she took a sip.

I said I guess.

Then she took a long gulp. Her swollen lips wrapped around the neck of the bottle. When she handed it back I could smell her clove saliva on the rim. I set the bottle aside for a while. It would have been rude to have wiped the rim clean after she had just taken a sip.

You're weird she said.

She said women don't like to be touched or bothered when they give birth.

I said I didn't know.

She said I'm not a Feel so it wasn't that bad.

She said you're a Smell aren't you.

Yeah I said.

She said I can tell because your place is so clean. Smells are always anal.

Huh I said.

Smells are always anal, Feels are always horny, Tastes are always fat, and Sounds are always paranoid she said.

I asked what she was.

She said I'm a Sight, so I'm curious and always spying and snooping.

I wish I was a Sight I said.

I'd rather be a Feel or a Taste she said.

I asked why.

She said they are more fun.

I said being a Smell is the worst.

It must be torturous in a place like this she said.

It has been I said.

She said at least you're clean. Feels and Smells are always the most attractive, because they take care of themselves. They don't like to smell or feel dirty.

She stretched her arms up and rested them on top of her head, releasing an assault of body odor from her wet armpits.

I only like to fuck Smells and Feels she said.

She looked me in the eyes and stepped forward, as if she could tell her armpit odor was offensive to me. I backed away from her.

She grabbed my bottle and chugged down the rest of the rice wine in one sip. She moved closer to me. I fell backwards onto the bed. She smirked and dropped the empty bottle next to me.

See you around she said.

Then she left my apartment.

I got up and followed her out of the room.

I'm Luci she said as she entered her apartment.

She lived right across the hall.

Lincoln I said.

See you around, Lincoln, she said.

Yeah I said.

I stood in the hallway with the door open for a few moments. Her smell was still in my apartment and I wanted to air it out a bit before reentering.

In the corner of my eyes I saw a short man walking down the hallway. I turned and looked at him. He was wearing a leather helmet and slamming his head into random doors, with an axe propped up on his shoulder. He didn't notice me. I decided to put up with Luci's lingering smell and go back into my apartment.

I locked the door and sat on my bed. The smell of clove and girl sweat was still strong in the air. I boiled some orange peels, hoping it would cover up the scent, but I only had one orange. So the room smelled like orange, clove, and girl sweat for the rest of the night.

The next morning I needed to go across town for art supplies. I got on the streetcar. It was mostly filled with people in Toyota uniforms. There were also a few Sonys, a Taco Bell, a Campbell's, and various other company uniforms I didn't recognize.

I sat down next to the woman in the Campbell's uniform. I didn't know much about the Campbell's people, but I knew they were nicer than most. Their corporation had been successful for so long that they didn't have very much competition, so they didn't need to promote competitiveness amongst their citizens. They didn't feel the need to promote hate and prejudice. Although the Campbell's woman wasn't likely to offer me friendship, she wasn't likely to show hostility either.

Ignoring the people around me, I watched the cityscape out of the window. The city was a maze of factories and tall old buildings. Everything was made of gray brick and wrought iron. All of the people we passed had sad, scared, angry faces.

At one of the stops, I saw a couple McDonald's recruiters on the sidewalk, catching six-month-old fetus flies with large nets.

Fetus flies were normally caught at six months, once they were the size of turkeys and didn't fly very well anymore. The recruiters bring them back to the company's nursery where they are raised until they learn to use their arms and legs.

Then their infancy is over and their childhood begins. They are put into the company's school system and taught the company's language, the company's laws, the company's religion, and begin company training. Many children will be given a basic position at age 6, which is usually light factory work. As they grow up, they will be promoted to more difficult jobs. Some of them move up the ranks, some of them are specialized, and some of them do menial labor for the rest of their lives.

The art store was small and hidden between the city's enormous Nike complex and the Corporate Trade Center in a small strip of businesses that weren't getting any customers.

The store was a fifth the size of the one at the GO, but it was eighty miles closer than the GO complex so it was the one I was going to use.

The owner was raised by the GO. All the art supply stores were branches of the GO. He was a tall old man with a Salvador Dali mustache. The tiny amount of hair on his head was parted in a ridiculous comb-over that had been dyed black. The black hair against his white scalp made him look like a zebra. Perhaps it was an artistic statement.

The man said you just starting your practice?

I nodded.

A newbie, eh?

The man raised his pointy eyebrows and winked.

I brought all of the paints, canvas paper, turpentine, and brushes that I was going to need to the counter.

I'll put this on your GO account he said.

I gave him my identification number.

He smiled and said happy creating.

I thought there was something too cheerful about this man. Perhaps pleasantries were a part of his job description.

I bought some PBR at the convenience store. Pabst was one of the few beer companies I was willing to give money to. Most beer companies, like Anheuser-Busch, had company laws that made it illegal for their people to drink alcohol. They didn't want their employees drinking their product and they didn't want them to drink any of their competitors' products either. The Pabst corporation didn't care, though. They let their employees drink all day long. They weren't the most successful beer company in the world, but they had the happiest and most loyal workers. If I had been raised by a company rather than an organization I would have wanted to be brought up by Pabst.

While walking down the hallway towards my apartment, that strong fig and raw hamburger smell attacked my nostrils. It was coming from under the doorway of the apartment next to mine. I hadn't caught the smell in the hallway before, but I was usually in a rush when I passed this apartment. The smell was putrid. It was also more complex than the smell had been when traveling through the cracks in the brick wall. The smell was not only like fig and raw hamburger meat, but also like ammonia, rotten bell peppers, dead earwigs, and water chestnuts.

I sniffed the air for a few minutes so that I could guess what the smell could possibly be coming from, but it eventually became too potent and I couldn't take much more of it. I went into my apartment and cleaned the place again until everything smelled like lemony chemicals.

In the morning I stretched some canvas and started on my first painting. I didn't know what to paint. The point of my practice was to develop a signature style. I had four years to blossom into a unique and worthwhile artist or else the GO would dump me. I really enjoyed doing abstract work, but they told me the style of abstract I was doing was nothing new. I had to come up with something completely different than anything I had ever done before. Something ground-breaking. Something bold.

I painted a cat.

There was a knock at the door and Luci entered. The door had been locked but she was able to get in anyway.

She said do you have any more of that wine, Lincoln?

It's nine in the morning I said.

So she said.

I said don't you have to go to work?

She said no.

I said I don't have anymore wine.

She said oh and turned to leave the room.

I have beer I said.

Okay she said.

She came into the room and shut the door. She went into my icebox and took out a PBR. Then she plopped down on my bed and watched me while she drank.

She said what are you doing?

My job I said.

What's your job?

I'm a painter.

Painter?

Well, a painter in training I said.

Oh she said.

I'm a citizen of the Georges Organization I said.

She said what's that?

I said it's a nonprofit organization that creates artists. They raise us in a creative environment and train us to become painters, actors, musicians, dancers, writers, stuff like that.

Why do they do that?

To enrich humanity I guess.

She said but they don't make money?

The artists that they raise go off into the world and make their livings selling their crafts. The organization gets a percentage of what the artists earn. They usually assist in this process. They have connections with galleries and music companies. The more talented you are the more they help you sell your work.

She said are you talented?

Not really I said.

Why?

I'm not a Sight. All the best artists are Sights. Just like all the best culinary artists are Tastes and all the best musicians are Sounds and all the best dancers are Feels. I'm just a smell. We don't have a specialty in the arts. The only reason I chose to be a painter was because I always liked the smell of paints when I was younger.

Luci said I'm a sight maybe I can help.

She stood up from the bed and went around my back.

It's a cat she said.

Yeah I said.

Kind of boring she said.

Yeah I said.

You're not very talented she said.

Yeah I said.

I decided to take a break from painting and have a beer with Luci. She didn't smell as bad as she did yesterday. She must have finally taken a bath. Maybe her sweat was just dry. Maybe the smell of the paint in the room was overpowering the body odor.

I sniffed close to her when she wasn't looking. She was definitely smelling better. The paint smell was strong but not strong enough to block any other scents. It didn't even block the fig and raw hamburger aroma that came through the brick wall.

I said what's with the person next door?

Luci drank her beer at me.

There's a horrible odor coming from that apartment I said.

We don't talk about it she said.

I said don't talk about what?

She drank her beer with nervous eyes.

That's where the Egg Man lives she said.

I said the what?

She said thanks for the beer.

Then she left.

After a PBR and a can of stew, I got back to work. I painted a distorted black and gray cityscape. It was pathetic. I liked painting non-objective abstracts. I liked swirling paint together and smelling it on my brush. I didn't like painting cats and landscapes. I drank another beer and thought about what I could do that was different from everything else out there. I was beginning to believe that creating something truly unique was impossible because everything has already been done.

My teachers always said that only a failed artist would ever believe that it's impossible to create something truly unique because everything has already been done. They said that this is just an excuse that unimaginative artists give themselves so that they don't have to try so hard to be original.

I drank the rest of the beers, hoping that the alcohol would be inspirational. It wasn't.

I decided to go out for some more beer but as soon as I opened the door to my apartment a short man came flying through the doorway and head-butted me with a leather helmet.

I fell to the ground. The helmet had split the skin on my forehead and I was bleeding a bit.

Oh sorry about that said the man.

He was holding an axe.

I said what the fuck?

He said are you okay?

Put the axe down I said.

45

Sorry said the man.

He put the axe down and took off his helmet. He had a round face, shaggy brown hair, thin black eyes, and a tiny mustache.

I held my wound and said what the fuck were you doing? Why do you feel the need to ram your head into doors?

I just do that to keep people on their toes said the man.

Why?

The man said people don't know what's out there. We live in a dangerous world. Their companies aren't always going to protect them. They need to know how to survive on their own.

I said and you're teaching them how to survive by hitting their doors with your head?

He said no I'm just keeping them on their toes. Staying on your toes is the first key to survival.

It's annoying I said.

It's worth getting annoyed when survival is at stake.

Annoy the wrong person and they'll kill you I said.

He said nobody would kill me. They need me.

I said why's that?

Let me show you he said.

The man, whose name turned out to be Squik, took me down the hall to his room. His apartment was much larger than mine. It was still one room but it was big enough for him to put up draperies that gave the illusion of walls.

I'll give you a free sample said Squik.

I said okay.

It's the least I could do after hitting you in the face said Squik.

He gave me a free sample. It was a little vial with two ounces of a tan fluid.

I said what is it?

The Squik Special. It'll blow your mind.

Maybe later I said, putting it into my pocket.

He said I've got a good little business going here, selling this stuff to the people in the neighborhood. I don't need a company to survive. I'm my own company. I've even got an apprentice.

I said apprentice?

Gordi he said.

From behind one of the curtains a five year old boy came out. He was wearing baggy adult-sized clothes and had a dirty expressionless face.

Squik said I found him in an alley and took him in just like the corporations do. He's a tough one. He was fifteen months old when I found him. Can you believe that he survived fifteen months out there on the streets?

I said it used to happen all the time. Centuries ago, before there were companies and organizations that raised our young, people had to survive all on their own.

Squik said exactly, it was the survival of the fittest. We weren't meant to be controlled by corporations. We were meant to be independent. Every man for himself.

I said yet you are taking care of a kid?

Squik said we help each other. He's a tough kid. He'd make it without me no problem. We're more like business partners.

The kid smiled with gritty blue teeth. He smelled like battery acid and sesame oil.

I tried to leave the apartment but Squik ran in front of me.

He said want a beer?

I said umm...

He gave me a beer.

I got stuck talking with Squik for over two hours. He rambled on about conspiracies and read his manifesto for how he could make the world a better place by tearing down the whole of civilization. He told me that he was a Sound. I hate stereotyping, but Luci was right. Sounds are paranoid.

I said do you know Luci?

Squik said stay away from her. She's a leech.

I said what's a leech?

She doesn't belong to a company anymore and she's not an independent like myself. She survives by leeching off of other people. She gets people to pay her rent, buy her things, give her money. She's worthless. Stay away from her.

I thought she was OSM I said.

He said yeah right. She couldn't work at the steel mill, even at the most basic position they've got. She was disenfranchised when she was thirteen. She doesn't know what a hard day's work is like.

She's always dirty and sweaty I said.

She's too lazy to take care of herself Squik said.

I said is she seeing anybody?

He said do you like her?

No I said. She's the grossest woman I've ever met.

Good he said.

But there's something attractive about her I said.

Squik said have you been listening? Stay away from her.

Okay I said.

What ever you do don't sleep with her Squik said.

I wasn't planning on it.

She's a no good leech he said.

Chapter #5

I decided to take Squik's advice and avoid Luci for a while. I had to go in front of the GO review board in a few days and present what I had been working on during the week. I heard the review board was tough. They didn't care about hurting your feelings. They told you exactly how terrible they thought your work was without an ounce of pity. They were the harshest critics I'd likely ever encounter. If I brought them paintings of cats and landscapes they were going to skin me alive, so I spent the next couple days focusing on originality.

I painted a tree that grew fruit shaped like pigs with human faces. It might have worked but the colors were all wrong. It was too rushed.

Then I painted a severed head that had factory machines draining out of the neck like blood. It didn't look too bad, but it didn't mean anything. If I had a message behind the drawing I might have liked it, but it's just a severed head with machinery. Perhaps I could pretend it's a statement on the cut-throat nature of the industrial world, but I didn't really know all that much about the industrial world. It didn't mean anything to me. I felt nothing for this painting. Still, it was the best one so far. At least the paintings were getting better.

Back when I was in school I had an instructor who said that if you don't know what to paint you should find inspiration from your memories. All I had to do was find a memory that stood out. The more recent the memory the better. All I had to do was freeze that memory into a still frame and paint the image in my head onto the canvas.

The most recent memory that came to mind was when I first arrived at the Henry Building and stepped into the half-dead fetus fly that was being eaten by ants. I wondered if that would make a good painting. I imagined what it would look like on canvas. A boot crushing a half dead fetus fly that was covered in ants. It was the best idea I had going, so I decided to go with that one.

I began the painting that night. I used pencil first. Normally I didn't outline the sketch first, but this was a little more complicated painting than I was used to doing. I decided to use a business executive's dress shoe instead of a steel-toed boot. That would probably make more of an impact on people.

While I was sketching, there was a gurgling noise coming from the west wall. A rumbling sound. It was the Egg Man.

I said what the hell is an egg man?

There was nobody around to answer.

The wall vibrated at me. The smell of fig and raw hamburger meat filled the room. I pressed my ear against the brick and listened. There were bubbling and gurgling noises. It was like I was listening to a giant stomach. The walls of the apartment were digesting the occupant within. There was a moan. It sounded like a dying elephant. Whatever was going on behind that wall wasn't natural. Whatever the Egg Man was, he wasn't human.

I finished the painting but I wasn't yet satisfied with it. The composition was perfect, the colors were fine, the subject was great, but something was missing.

I needed another set of eyes to help me figure it out. The only people I knew in the apartment were Luci and Squik. I told Squik I wouldn't talk to Luci anymore, but Luci would be perfect because she was a Sight. Squik was only a Sound and he would have probably talked my ear off for hours if I invited him over. I decided not to go to Squik.

I went across the hall and knocked on Luci's door.

Come in she said.

I went in.

The smells of her apartment were potent. Before I even saw anything, I could smell month-old dirty dishes, year-old dirty laundry, body odor, ash trays, molds, mildew, sour milk, vomit, and old beer. The apartment was identical to mine but there wasn't any furniture. She had a mattress on the floor. A toilet. A sink. That was about it. She had clothes everywhere and her floor was covered in dozens of different colored stains.

Luci was topless. She was washing her white tank top with a bar of soap in her kitchen sink. The sink was filled with dirty dishes, so I wasn't sure if her shirt was getting cleaner or more disgusting.

I stood just inside of the room, watching the dim lighting glisten off the sweat on her creamy cocoa-colored back. She turned and looked at me. I could see the side of her breast, but not the nipple.

Oh it's you she said.

She turned around and put on her wet shirt. She didn't seem to mind exposing her bare chest. I tried not to let on that I had seen her breasts so I quickly looked to the side and noticed she had a tub in her room. It was an old metal tub, basically just a big bucket that had to be filled and emptied by hand.

You have a tub I said.

Yeah she said.

I don't have a tub I said.

You can use it if you need to she said.

Maybe I said.

She said is that why you came over?

I said no I wanted your help with something. Can you give me your opinion on the painting I'm working on?

Sure she said.

Back in my apartment, I showed her the painting of the half-dead fetus fly.

I said what do you think?

She said I don't like it.

I wasn't expecting such honesty.

It's too two-dimensional she said. It doesn't have any depth or the right texture.

I said depth?

Examining it for a moment, I said I see what you mean.

It needs to *pop* she said.

Her fingers snapped out of her fist at me when she said *pop*.

Pop? I said.

Pop she said.

I said I think I undersand . . . Thanks.

She said no problem.

I stared at the painting for a while, considering what I could do to add texture and depth to the image.

She said want to fuck now?

I stepped away. Remembering Squik's warning, I had to figure out a way to reject her without hurting her feelings.

She took off her shirt and grabbed me by the neck. Then sucked my tongue between her fat glossy lips and swallowed my saliva. Her tongue tasted like clove, but the smell of her sweat and dirty ratty hair overpowered my sense of taste. After I couldn't take the smell anymore, I pushed her away. She giggled and looked at me as if she knew exactly why I pushed her away. She came towards me and I held her shoulders back. She smiled at me, like I was just being flirtatious.

She pulled my shirt off and gasped in excitement when she noticed the wings on my back.

She said you still have your wings?

Yeah I said.

She said that's so cute!

I felt her fingers caressing my wings behind me.

I said the GO doesn't cut our wings off while we're still fetus flies like most of the corporations do.

She said do they work?

I flapped my wings for her. She giggled.

She said can you fly with them?

I said not really. If I took all of my clothes off and lost a few pounds I could get about ten feet off the ground for a couple minutes. That's about all.

They're neat she said.

They're a pain I said.

She said I'm definitely going to have to fuck you now. I've never had anyone with wings before.

I didn't know what else to do. I wanted to push her away, but she was too aggressive. And even though she was so dirty and smelled terrible, she was still incredibly attractive.

Let's take a bath first I said.

No she said.

Come on I said.

She laughed. She took off her pants and then pulled down mine.

It gets me hot when you smell me she said.

You smell like body odor I said.

I know she said.

She rubbed her moist body against mine, saturating me with her smell. She took sweat from her armpit and wiped it under my nose.

Body odor is an aphrodisiac she said.

I cringed at her and wiped my nose.

The scent of our sweat is designed to attract the opposite sex she said.

She licked sweat from my chest. I wasn't sure if it was mine, hers, or a mixture of both.

You're a Smell so it effects you intensely she said.

I shook my head at her.

She said you might think the odor is unpleasant, but the chemicals inside of your head are going wild right now. Your nose is repulsed by me but the rest of you is drawn to me. Now that I have my scent on you your body is *aching* for me. She wiped her hand down my chest and grabbed onto my penis. It was already hard. I hadn't noticed until she seized it.

As we fucked on my tiny bed, she forced me to smell her. She buried my nose in her armpit and ordered me to lick it. I was getting sick and wanted to stop, but my erection compelled me to bear with it. Every part of her body reeked of old sweat. Even her breasts. I tried to kiss her so that the taste of her smoky clove saliva would dull my sense of smell, but she wouldn't let me. She didn't want me to do anything but smell her as she fucked me.

She bit one of my wings and I cried out. She liked to hear me cry so she tugged on it with her teeth until I cried again.

When she came she wrapped her body tightly around mine and scrunched one of my wings in her hand. I shrieked grabbed her wrist with all of my strength, cutting her skin open with my fingernails. She liked it, though, and wouldn't loosen her grasp on the wing.

After she was done she caressed my wing and flattened it back into its original shape. She blew on it and fucked me gently as I came inside of her.

I could smell my semen inside of her as we lay together. If she were fertile then every single one of my sperms would grow inside of her, and her womb would mutate them into fetus flies that were a combination of our DNA.

I said what was it like to give birth the other day?

She said it was like taking a weird dump.

I said were you scared the first time you gave birth?

She said it was actually fun giving birth back then.

She said when I was a teenager, my girlfriends and I used to play birthing games. We used to put fly paper up on the wall and spread our legs around it. Once we'd given birth and released the swarm, a lot of them would get stuck to the fly paper. We made a bet to see who could stick the most fetus flies to their fly paper within a year's time. I won a couple times.

That's pretty cruel I said.

Big deal she said.

She said we also used to give birth over camp fires so the fetus flies would ignite in midair. I also had a friend who would release her fetus flies into an aquarium of frogs. She liked to watch the frogs catch her tiny babies with their long sticky tongues and slurp them down one by one.

That's terrible I said.

She said we were kids. That's what little girls do.

I never heard of any of that before I said.

It's just for fun she said.

I said are you going to do that with our babies?

She said what are you talking about? Do you think I'm going to have your babies now or something?

I shrugged.

She said you've never had sex before.

I said so?

She said how old are you?

Nineteen I said.

You're just a baby she said.

How old are you?

Thirty-one she said.

I thought you were more like twenty-one I said.

No, thirty-one.

Huh I said.

No wonder why you're so sexually passive she said.

Luci fell asleep on me. I couldn't sleep because I was saturated in her smell. I smelled like her now. Our smells had combined into one. The bed was too small for us to sleep side by side so she slept on top of me. My wings were being crushed behind my back.

The west wall rumbled and gurgled. The vibration startled Luci and woke her up. She looked nervously at the wall. It sloshed and thundered at her.

She rolled over me and fell onto the floor. Without saying a word she sprinted out of my apartment naked and went back to hers. The rumbling sounds subsided after she left.

Chapter
#6

I had only one day left before I had to go in front of the review board. I needed to figure out a way to add depth to the painting. I tried adding contrast by putting very light colors against very dark colors but it didn't seem to help. I went outside to see if I could find a dead fetus fly somewhere for reference and inspiration.

On the steps in front of the Henry Building I discovered the football-sized fetus fly that I had stepped into was still there. It was dead and had been brushed off of the steps into the dirt. It was dried out and looked hollow inside. Ants were no longer interested in it.

I picked up the dead fetus fly with a McDonald's burger wrapper that was crumpled up on the side of the road. Then I brought it up to my apartment. It still smelled. Though I didn't want its smell in my room, I was desperate enough to put up with it. I was already putting up with the leftovers of Luci's stink, so it didn't bother me as much as it normally would have.

Propping the dead fetus fly up like a still life, I went back to painting. After an hour, I screamed at the canvas. I still couldn't get the depth right. It needed texture, but capturing the texture of the fetus fly was difficult. I'd never tried to paint rotted flesh before.

Out of frustration I slammed my brush into the fetus fly over and over again. Its tiny body crumbled and broke apart on the table. I calmed myself and went back to painting. Bits of dead fetus skin were still on the brush and got inside of the picture.

I said hmmm . . .

Incorporating real dead flesh in with the paint actually seemed to give the painting an interesting texture. I crushed the fetus fly up into crumbs and mixed it with my paint. I painted a new fetus fly over the one in the picture. When I was finished, the image startled me. It seemed to jump off of the canvas at me. It looked like a real dead thing and it smelled like one too. I believed this one was good enough to show the review board, even if the others were not. Though none of my paintings were brilliant, they did show how much my skill had progressed from one painting to the next. It was only the first week of my practice. If they didn't like what I had created they would at least see a slight glimmer of potential.

The next day I asked Luci if she could help me carry my paintings to the streetcar. I didn't have a portfolio case yet so transporting my artwork was a real hassle.

She said sure.

As we walked, she giggled and called me a bug.

They are like dragonfly wings she said about my wings.

You had them too I said.

She said but I got them removed like normal people do.

I knew she was only being flirtatious. She smiled and admired my fetus fly painting while we walked.

It turned out pretty good she said.

Squik was totally wrong about Luci. She didn't seem like a leech at all. She was a nice girl, under her dirt and stink.

I said why did you leave my room the other night?

She said your bed is crap.

I said you saw my wall rumbling. It was like you got scared of the Egg Man.

So she said.

I said what is the Egg Man?

I don't know she said.

She paused for a moment.

I only know the stories she said.

What stories?

They say he's like the boogey man. He's a hideous monster of a man who has been living in room 314 ever since the Henry Building was first built. They say he never leaves his apartment because he's too large. They had to build the walls around him. He survives by eating children and dogs. His lungs are so powerful that he can suck a child playing in the street up into the air, through his window, and then he swallows them whole.

I said like feeding fetus flies to a frog.

She said I don't know anyone who has actually seen the Egg Man. The stories have been passed through the building for years. Some people say that nobody lives in apartment 314. They think that the Egg Man is some kind of ghost. Everyone hears noises inside of the apartment. Everyone can smell something coming from behind the door. But nobody has entered or left that apartment in years. Something unnatural is inside of there and I don't like being anywhere near it.

After Luci dropped me off at the corner, she said you can return the favor another time.

I said okay.

I didn't know whether to hug her goodbye, kiss her goodbye, or shake her hand. Before I could make a decision, she turned around walked away without bothering with a goodbye.

The streetcar took an extra long time getting there. It was supposed to be the most reliable form of public transportation, but not on that day. While I was waiting, I witnessed a man and a woman, both in red jumpsuits, get gunned down in the middle of the street. The shooters were five men in gray OSM uniforms. They fled from the scene of the crime in my direction, nearly knocking me over as they ran.

For some reason, I wasn't worried about getting shot. I was more worried about them damaging my paintings. I shielded them with my body, but the murderers still knocked one of them out of my arms by accident. It was the painting of the cat, which fell face-first onto the pavement with a loud smack. I picked it up. The bottom edge of the canvas was dented but it was fine. Of all the paintings, it was the only one I would have been okay with losing.

Nobody did anything about the dead couple in the

red uniforms. Their bodies remained where they were, leaking blood onto the sidewalk. By the end of the day, their bodies would still be there, but their blood would be tracked up and down the street as passersby casually stepped through it without taking much notice.

It might take days, but eventually a company would claim the bodies of their dead citizens and bury them in the company graveyard (if burying is their company's policy on death).

I arrived at the GO complex a little behind schedule. The review board was known to be extremely pissy about tardiness. People always used to say that getting to the review board for your weekly meeting on time was more important than bringing a decent painting.

I had to run from the streetcar through the black dirt park in front of the GO complex, trying to hold my five paintings together. The pig tree painting slipped out of my hand and landed in the dirt. I grabbed it and continued on, but didn't have enough time to wipe it off.

I went up to the seventh floor of the education building, which was one of the few floors I had never been on. There were three board members waiting impatiently at a table. There were five seats behind the table, but two of them were empty. I wasn't a high prospect so they probably didn't need all five board members there. One of them was an old man with a droopy chin. One of them was a stocky man with a full beard. One of them was a middle-aged woman with short red hair, a gray business suit, and eyebrows that touched the top of her forehead.

The old man saw me and pointed at the empty chair that was facing them on the other side of the table.

We don't have all day said the woman in an obnoxiously loud tone.

I rushed towards the chair.

Over here said the bearded man with a gruff voice, waving me towards him. He sat in the middle of the table, so he must have been the one with the most authority.

I realized he wanted my paintings. They were sloppily smashed together. Running across the lot probably damaged some of them.

The woman said well these aren't going to be very good if the artist doesn't even like them enough to take care of them.

I handed them to the bearded man. He seemed bored. He spread the paintings out across their table. The three board members glanced across the table with little interest.

The old man looked through my file. He said you're not a Sight, are you?

No I said.

Figures said the woman.

I'm a Smell I said.

A lot of the older people in the art community believed that only Sights could be great artists. I really wished the fact that I was a Smell hadn't come up.

They examined the paintings carefully.

The woman said crap . . . crap . . . crap . . . as she looked through the paintings.

The bearded man laughed out loud twice.

You like cats I see said the woman, in an obviously condescending tone.

Yeah I said.

I have two cats said the woman. I used to paint cats all the time . . . as a child.

That painting was just for warm up, to break in my new paint brushes I said.

She said if it was just a practice painting then why did you bother bringing it to us? Don't waste our time with nonsense. We only want to see your best.

The bearded man was done looking at my paintings and closed his eyes. His arms folded across his chest.

The woman said are *all* of these practice paintings? They all look like *practice* if you ask me.

She held up my fetus fly painting and said was this supposed to be a serious work of art?

She put it down and held up the pig tree painting.

She said or how about this one? Was this dirt brushed across the surface of the painting for artistic effect or did you drop it on the ground on your way here?

There was a ball in the back of my throat. I wanted to defend my work but I feared that if I tried to speak I would instead cry.

The old man pointed at the paintings the old woman

had and they swapped the arrangement of them so that she could see the ones that were on the old man's side of the table.

She gave the last two paintings two seconds before she developed an opinion of them.

She said how long did it take you to paint these two? Ten minutes?

The woman stared at me as if she really wanted a reply.

I just shrugged at her because I didn't know what else to do.

She said are you satisfied with any of these? Which one do you think is the best?

I took a deep breath before I spoke so that my voice wouldn't crack.

The fetus fly one I said.

The old man raised it over his head and said this one?

I nodded.

The old man said what is it called?

I didn't have a title for it so I made one up.

Work Day I said.

The old man said softly can you explain it for us?

I said it's a picture of a business man crushing a pathetic dying fetus fly under his shoe on his way to the office.

The woman said but what's it mean?

I said it's a statement about the self-centeredness of Man. The weakest and most helpless of us are crushed by the rich and powerful on a day to day basis. It is about the hopelessness of survival in a world where the powerful don't care for those they crush under foot.

Oh wonderful said the woman in an energetic burst of sarcasm.

I knew that what I had said was a bunch of improvised bullshit but the woman's snobbish tone was really getting under my skin.

Well . . . said the old man.

He was still examining the fetus fly painting.

The old man said the explanation isn't any good . . . the composition isn't any good . . . the colors are weak . . . the concept isn't anything new . . . but . . .

He paused for a moment.

But there is something really powerful here said the old man.

The woman laughed out loud.

I couldn't tell if the old man was being sarcastic or not.

It's the smell of it said the old man.

The woman said the smell?

The old man said he's not a Sight. He's not good with his eyes. He's a Smell, so he painted with his nose instead.

That's the stupidest thing I've ever heard said the woman.

The bearded man closed his eyes and took a sniff at the painting.

The old man said I want to get Koonce in here. He's a Smell. I'd like a Smell to analyze this.

Koonce isn't on this board said the woman.

Koonce has been on the committee for nearly thirty-five years said the old man. I trust his opinion more than most review board members, especially with a painting that involves smell.

I finally started to believe that the old man was being serious. He actually saw a glimmer of hope for my work. Not because of the look of my painting, but because of the smell of it.

Ten minutes later a man with a small head, a white goatee, and large gray teeth stepped into the review chamber.

The old man showed Koonce my painting. The goateed man examined it and sniffed at it. He rubbed his chin.

It's actually quite impressive said Koonce. It's perhaps the most disturbing painting I've ever seen. Visually, it's simple and lacks power but the smell overwhelms me. You can almost sense the frustration in the tiny creature's mind as it rots alive. A Sight probably wouldn't care for this piece much, but I bet there'd be a big market for this out there for Smells.

The woman said Smells don't buy art. Smells don't know how to appreciate art.

I'm sure Smells could appreciate artwork that they

could smell said Koonce.

The bearded man looked very interested in the painting after Koonce had given his opinion.

The bearded man looked up at me and said can you do another one?

Yes I said.

Bring us one more next week said the bearded man. We're out of time so we'll discuss this further at a later date.

The old man said just focus on one painting. Give us something with passion. Put your soul into it.

Give us something that Smells would be interested in said the bearded man.

The woman said and next time if you don't have an explanation for a piece don't make something up on the spot. No explanation is always better than a feeble one.

Chapter #7

When I got home I was in the mood to celebrate. My success with the review board was a complete fluke, but it went over superbly nonetheless.

I knocked on Luci's door with a couple of bottles of rice wine. She didn't answer. I knocked again.

I said where the heck could she be?

I thought she never went anywhere or did anything.

Then I went down the hall to Squik's apartment and decided to celebrate with him.

Squik said congratulations and took a swig of my rice wine.

Thanks I said with rice wine in my mouth.

He said so how did you like the Squik Special?

I said oh I haven't had time to try it yet.

Squik said I gave you a free sample you have to try it.
Okay I said.

Gordi was mixing a vat of Squik's special in the
corner. His shirt was off, revealing dozens of horrible
scars. It looked as if he got them a long time ago, when he
was a fetus fly. Or maybe they were more recent. There
were sticks of flesh on his back where his wings used to
be. Whoever cut them off didn't do a very good job of it.
I first guessed that Squik was the one who had cut them
off, but on closer inspection it looked more like Gordi
had done the job himself.

I said have you seen Luci?

He said you haven't been hanging out with Luci have
you?

I said kinda.

He said damn, don't be an idiot, man.

I shrugged.

He said you didn't fuck her did you?

I shrugged.

He said you did, didn't you? Man, you have no idea
what you've done. She's a leech. She fucks guys just so
she can sink her fangs into them. If you keep fucking her
she will bleed you dry.

I said she's not like that.

He said she's an expert leech. She's known how to
survive as a leech since she was thirteen.

I said I don't know, she's gross but I kind of like
her.

He said what do you think you're going to be her
boyfriend or something?

I shrugged.

He said she probably has a dozen boyfriends in this apartment alone. One of them from upstairs thinks he owns her and goes after any guy that she fucks. He's OSM. You don't want him on your bad side. If one OSM sees you as an enemy all of the OSMs will.

I said I don't want to be her boyfriend.

He said but you're going to fuck her again, huh?

I said I don't get a lot of sex. A leech girl is better than no one.

He said you can fuck any other girl you want.

I said I'm not very lucky with women.

He said how many have you slept with?

I shrugged.

He said you weren't a virgin when you fucked her were you?

I didn't know how to lie to him.

He said oh fuck, really? Fuck.

I took a long swig of the wine.

He said you didn't tell her you were a virgin did you?

Yeah I said.

He said damn, you're doomed, man. You're doomed. She will enslave you with her pussy. Then she will bleed you dry. She's an expert leech. She knows when she's found a fat juicy prey that's easy to milk.

I'm not an idiot I said.

He said you'll sure feel like one after she's done with you.

I asked Squik about the Egg Man. I told him the stories Luci had told me.

I said are they true?

Heck no he said.

Fucking dumb bitch Squik said.

I said then what's in apartment 314.

Squik said Ralph lives there. He's one of those egg heads.

I said what are egg heads?

Squik said egg head is actually a slur. You don't want to call him the Egg Man to his face. It'll piss him off.

He took a swig of wine.

He said egg heads have these massive brains that can get up to ten times or twenty times the weight of their actual body. Some egg heads have rods and pulleys rigged up to hold their head in the air. Most of them have heads so large that they can't even leave their apartments, like Ralph.

He said they are disgusting, but perfectly harmless.

I said are they mutants or something?

Squik said they aren't born with mega-brains. Their company implants the mega-brain into them.

I said for what purpose?

He said the mega-brains store company information. They don't need to keep paper records anymore, they can just upload their records into an egg head's brain.

I said what happens if the egg head dies?

He said many egg heads are hooked up to machines that manage their health. The machines will keep them alive for fifty years longer than an average human. If the human dies the machines are still able to save the brain and preserve it until the information can be passed on to a new host.

I said how do you know all of this?

He said I'm a Sound. I'm in the know.

I didn't know what being a Sound had to do with it.

He said besides, egg heads are all over the place. I'm surprised you haven't heard of them before. I always used to see them walking around the streets with their enormous 15-foot brains hovering above them.

I said they can carry something that big?

He said yeah, I remember the brains were always sopping with sweat and smelled terrible. Fetus flies would get stuck to the sides of their heads. Spiders would build webs in the folds of the brain.

I said who the hell would ever want to go through that?

He said some people get implanted as kids and their company doesn't give them a choice. Others are paid a considerable amount of money.

I said there's no amount of money anyone could pay me to go through that all my life.

I listened to the gurgling and bubbling noises coming through the wall as I slept that night, imagining what the Egg Man looked like in his apartment next door. His brain was so big that he couldn't ever leave his apartment. His life must have been a living hell.

I wondered what painting I should do next. It had to be something powerful. Something much better than the dead fetus fly. Thinking back to my recent memories, only one image stuck out in my mind: Luci giving birth in the street.

That might work I said.

A painting of a dirty impoverished woman giving birth in the street could make a strong image. Incorporating the smells of that scene would make it even stronger.

I hoped to get started on it right away.

I went to Luci's to tell her about how I wanted to paint a picture of when she gave birth.

She wanted me to buy some drugs from Squik so

that we could fuck while tripping.

I told her I already had a free sample.

We did Squik's Special and then she fucked me in a pile of dirty clothes.

The drug made me smell colors and textures.

I smelled Luci's colors and textures as she fucked me.

The light brown color of her skin smelled like apricots.

The texture of her hair smelled like grape leaves.

The plumpness of her breasts smelled like powdered wood.

After we came, we enjoyed the drug until it faded away.

I said I'd like you to pose for me.

She twirled her pubic hair with an index finger.

I'll pay you I said.

She was happy to pose for me, for money.

She said will I be naked?

I said it should be like how it was that day.

She said I don't remember.

You didn't have any pants on I said.

She took off her pants.

I planned to paint the street and the fetus flies later. It was important to get down Luci's form while she was willing to be a model.

I painted Luci in a squatting position, the way she was when she gave birth. Her belly wasn't swollen anymore so I asked her to push it out as far as she could.

With the edge of a ruler, I scraped globs of Luci's sweat from her thighs and mixed it with the paint.

Then I mixed the sweat on her back into another paint. I used the sweat on her face to paint her face. I used the sweat on her arms to paint her arms. I had her spit onto my brush to give a clove flavor to her lips. I collected samples of her armpit smell, her feet smell, her crotch smell.

She said you have to get my ass sweat too.

I wiped up a gobbet of slime from her ass crack to paint her asshole. Her asshole wasn't really showing in the picture but I decided to humor her by putting a little sliver of ass sweat along the rim of her painting's butt cheek.

Getting the smell of her shirt and hair weren't as easy. I had to water them down and then wring them out into cups. The water diluted the smells, but it was the best I could do.

It took a couple of days of painting and repainting, but eventually I got Luci perfect.

When the paint was dry, I inspected the image of her body with my nose. A slight smell of the paint was in the background, but otherwise her scent was perfect. The visual representation of her might not have been perfect, but the smell of it was like Luci was standing right there in the room with me.

The only problem was that it didn't smell the same as when she was actually giving birth. I had to figure out a way to recapture that flavor.

Chapter #8

One night, a large man with a shaved head and gray skin slammed open my door.

At first, I thought it was Squik, but when I saw the OSM uniform I realized who it was.

He said I heard you're fucking my bitch.

He charged through the room and grabbed me by the shirt.

She's my bitch he said.

Spit sprayed across my forehead.

He said nobody fucks her but me.

I prayed he didn't discover Luci's image in the painting behind him. If he saw it he probably would have smashed it.

He threw me to the ground and kicked me in the stomach with his work boots.

He said fuck her again and you're dead.

Then he left.

Squik shook his head at me after I told him what had happened.

He said I told you.

I said what am I going to do?

He said stop fucking Luci.

I said it's not that easy. She comes after me. I've never pursued her. Now I need her for my painting.

He said you better watch out. OSM doesn't have any laws against murdering people outside of the company.

GO does I said.

You need protection he said.

Like what?

He gave me a hunting knife.

He said your organization won't protect you. Nobody in this world will help you but you. If he threatens you again you kill him before he kills you. You need to be a survivor. You need to be able to defend yourself.

I said what if he has a gun?

Then you need to get a gun he said.

I decided I would only see Luci while the OSMs were at work. She came over the next day and we got into the painting. I wanted to add another layer of Luci's sweat. Instead of paint, I mixed the sweat into a finishing gloss.

While I was collecting her smell there was a gurgling and rumbling sound at the west wall. Luci broke her pose and ran out of the room. I followed her across the hall into her apartment.

I can't do it anymore she said.

She was flustered.

Calm down I said.

I can't handle hearing it anymore she said.

I said don't worry, don't worry.

I sat her down on the bed. It was soggy for some reason and smelled of beer. I told her what Squik had told me about the Egg Man. It took her a while but her fear eventually subsided.

She said really?

I said yeah.

But how does he eat? Nobody brings him food.

I don't know I said.

After that, Luci's fear turned into curiosity.

We were up on the roof of the condemned building across the street. Luci was using her strong sense of sight to peer through the Egg Man's window.

I said see anything?

She said not yet.

She was focusing her eyes and trying to make out what was beyond the sunlight that reflected against the window glass.

Fuuuuuck she said.

What?

I think something is moving in there she said.

What?

It's big she said.

She laughed.

What?

There was a big smile on her face.

You were right she said.

She squinted her eyes.

He's disgusting she said.

I tried to see it with my own eyes but everything was a blur beyond the glass of the window.

She said he's fucking scary.

Then she ducked as if the creature had spotted her. She giggled into my chest.

She said he is the grossest most deformed thing I have ever seen.

I said what does he look like?

He is just a giant head. He has a dead bloated walrus for a head.

She giggled more and raced down the ladder like she was embarrassed of what she had just done.

Luci and I walked through the street.

Massive spider webs like canopies stretched across the street from building to building overhead. There weren't any spiders that I could see, but there were several dead fetus flies in them. We wondered if any of the fetus flies were Luci's.

I bought us sandwiches from the convenience store and we ate them in our laps on the sidewalk.

After that, I collected smells for my painting and put them into plastic bags. I scraped powder off of the pavement and the street. I picked tiny dead fetus flies out of spider webs and windowsills. I collected rain water from a puddle to paint the atmosphere.

I said what else was there?

Huh Luci said.

She screwed up her eyebrows in thought.

Paper towels she said.

We went to the spot where Luci had given birth. The paper towels were still there on the side of the street.

I said I didn't actually paint in the paper towels though. I have you sitting with your bare butt against the sidewalk. It's more poetic that way.

Examining the paper towels, I noticed that Luci's afterbirth was covering the package. It was a thick black goo that still looked a little moist even though it had been there for several days.

You *have* to get some of that she said.

She was right. It was exactly what I needed to make the smell of the painting complete.

It's perfect I said.

I collected some of the black goo into a baggy.

Luci said can you get me some more drugs from Squik?

Sure I said.

As we were getting back to the Henry Building we saw a bunch of OSM people crowded in the front.

I said what are they doing back from the mill so early?

She said I don't know.

I didn't see the bald guy but if he saw me walking with Luci I was a dead man.

I said I'll go get the stuff from Squik and see you later.

She said okay.

I broke away from Luci and picked up the pace so that none of the OSM people thought I was with her.

Then I went up the stairs to see Squik.

Squik said did you hear what's happening?

No I said.

He said war has broken out between OSM and MSM.

I said MSM?

He said it's their rival steel company, which means this neighborhood is going to turn into a warzone. The mill is just a few blocks away from here and most of its workers live within a five block radius. The Henry Building is going to be a prime target.

I said I thought the United Corporations were working to end bloodshed between rival companies.

He said the UC is worth crap.

I said are we going to be safe?

He said not at all. We're going to be right in the middle of it. MSM is much stronger than OSM. They have been breeding their own army for the past twenty years and are now ready to make their move to dominate the steel industry. OSM will be slaughtered. We just have to make sure that we don't go down with them.

Fuck I said.

He said we need to arm ourselves. I'll get us some fire power. You got my back?

Sure I said.

Then I'll get you a gun he said.

I said hey can I buy some of your special?

Oh yeah Squik said.

He went to his lab and fixed me up with a vial.

He said Luci asked you to get it, didn't she?
Yeah I said.
Of course she did he said.

I finished my painting. The fetus flies were smelling like fetus flies. The birth was smelling like a birth. Luci smelled like Luci. The street smelled like a street. The air smelled like the air.

I got Luci from across the hall and asked for her opinion.

She stared at it and sniffed it.

Beautiful she said.

I wasn't sure if she was talking about my painting or her image within the painting.

She said the smell of it seems like it is probably perfect. It's visually stunning as well.

I was so happy with it that I kissed Luci on the cheek. When I pulled my lips back I felt powdered dead skin cells coating my lips and nose.

The west wall of my apartment rumbled and gurgled as we were tripping on Squik's Special.

I want to see what he looks like Luci said.

She pointed at the wall.

I said the Egg Man?

She nodded.

I said I thought you already saw him.

She said I want to see him close up.

I said how?

She said let's sneak into his place.

I said now?

Yeah.

I said we're tripping. You really want to sneak in there and meet that freak in this state?

She said yeah, it'll be a rush.

I don't want to I said.

She said what are you afraid of? Even if he gets angry he won't be able to chase us with that big head of his.

I guess I said.

Luci picked the lock on apartment 314 and opened the door. All she needed to pick the lock was a needle and a penny.

When the door opened, a wave of fatty odor oozed into the hallway. I plugged my nose and Luci laughed at me. Inside, the room was like none of the other apartments. There were machines of black iron against the walls. There were tubes all over the floor and pipes stretching up to the ceiling. The pipes leaked a thin smoke that smelled of ammonia and water chestnuts.

There was a large pulsating mass of gray flesh centering the apartment. It took up most of the room. It was the size of a whale or as Luci said, a walrus. It was the Egg Man's head.

His body was on the little bed. There were ropes and rods and straps holding the enormous head off of the ground.

The man's breath was loud and raspy. Large blue veins popped out of his skin. The whale of flesh was leaning against the wall that faced my apartment. There were gurgling sounds and rumbling vibrations coming from within his egg-shaped skull. His tiny yellow eyes rolled towards us.

Come in if you must he said in a phlegm-clogged voice.

We came in and shut the door.

His mutant flesh twisted and pulsed within our tripping visions.

I said I'm sorry we were just curious.

Luci stepped closer. I didn't want to get too close because of the smell.

Luci said can I touch it?

Gently he said.

Luci leaned over his body and placed her hand on his clammy throbbing brain.

It's so soft she said.

Her breasts were shoved into the Egg Man's face. Her body odor must have been overwhelming to him at that distance but he wasn't grossed out. He seemed to like it.

I said what's it like, having the oversized brain?

He said it's hard to explain how it feels. It is like having another world inside of your head.

I said isn't it painful and boring lying here all day long?

Luci continued feeling his brain as I spoke to him.

The Egg Man said as I just told you, I have another world inside of my head. I spend most of my time within that world.

Luci said what is the world like?

It is Heaven said the Egg Man.

Luci said what is Heaven?

The Egg Man said I am not your usual mega-brain. I am employed by Heaven, Inc. It is a company that sells the afterlife to the executive class.

I said what do you mean?

He said Heaven is the name of a virtual world that exists inside of mega-brains such as myself. Heaven, Inc. promises life after death. If you are rich enough to afford it you can have your soul transferred into Heaven before your death. In Heaven, you can live forever within a virtual paradise. A paradise that exists inside of my brain.

Luci put her ear to his brain and said there are souls inside of here?

Hundreds of thousands of them said the Egg Man.

A lot of companies had their own personal religions that they forced upon their workers. Some of these religions preached of an afterlife, a heaven. Most of these heavens were personalized and revolved around their company's culture. The McDonald's Heaven, for instance, was supposed to be a great playground in the sky where you would get to meet Ronald McDonald, Grimace, Mayor McCheese, and the fry guys. You could also eat as much McDonalds as you wanted and never gain a pound.

The GO taught me that most of these company religions were designed to brainwash their workers and that the people at the top didn't actually believe in any of it. The government of McDonald's knew that Ronald McDonald was a fictional character.

But the heaven inside of the Egg Man wasn't fiction. It was technology. Heaven Inc. created a real afterlife that people could buy if they were privileged enough.

Luci said can you interact with them in your brain?

I am like their god said the Egg Man.

Chapter #9

It was time to meet with the review board again. I asked Luci if I could use her bathtub. She said no because she had diarrhea, so I cleaned myself as best as I could in my sink.

Outside of the Henry Building there were a bunch of OSMs smoking cigarettes and chatting. They didn't seem to be worried about hanging out in public even though they were at war with a rival company. I wondered if the rumor was true. Squik didn't seem to be a reliable source of information.

There were six people in the review chamber this time, but the bitchy red-haired woman wasn't one of them.

The bearded man and the old man introduced me to Mr. Yates, a Smell who was also a gallery owner, Mrs. Normil who was on the scholarship board, Mr. Shang who was one of the review board members who was absent at the last meeting, and Mr. Koonce who I had already met. I still didn't know the names of the bearded man and the old man. They didn't care to introduce themselves at the last meeting.

I gave them my painting of Luci.

The old man said what is it called?

I haven't titled it yet I said.

I sat down in the chair and let the board examine the painting on their own. They conversed with each other about it. I couldn't hear what they were saying. I watched as the two Smells, Mr. Koonce and Mr. Yates, sniffed at the painting. They were appalled by the smells. Koonce looked like he was about to throw up. I wondered if I went a little overboard with Luci's stink.

After they were finished they took their seats and addressed me.

This one is very impressive said the bearded man. You have especially attracted the attention of Mr. Yates.

Mr. Yates said the smells are incredibly complex and powerful. There is a lot of emotion here. Not just in what you see but in what you smell.

It is life at its most disgusting said the old man, smiling.

I smiled back.

The bearded man said Mr. Yates is very interested in your work. If the quality of your paintings does not diminish then you might just have a future as a top artist.

The old man said Mr. Yates is already discussing the possibility of giving you a show once you have a strong body of work. He believes he can build a Smell clientele just for you.

The bearded man said we'd like you to do another one over the next week. I still think you are too rough but Mr. Yates believes he can sell your style of work. So I am reluctant to say that you will now be on the list of high prospects. Congratulations, you are the first Smell to ever obtain this privilege. We will set you up with a larger apartment uptown and increase your grant by three hundred percent.

I was in shock. This wasn't what I was expecting to hear.

Then I thought about it.

I said wait a minute.

They looked at me.

I can't move out of the Henry Building I said.

The bearded man said why not?

It's where I get my inspiration I said.

The bearded man said very well, you can live wherever you want.

I'm not sure why I was hesitant to accept the offer of a nicer apartment. The Henry Building was a shit hole.

I wondered: Was it because of Luci? Is she my inspiration? Or do I not want to move away because I'm falling in love with her?

I thought about that as I took the streetcar home. I wasn't sure if I even liked Luci but I also couldn't handle the idea of moving away from her.

When I got back to the Henry Building I broke open a bottle of rice wine and went across the hall to celebrate. I knocked on Luci's door. She didn't answer. I called her name. She wasn't there.

I could smell her body odor in the hallway, so I sniffed the air to figure out where it led. There was a trail of her scent from her apartment to apartment 314, where the trail ended. I smelled the door to room 314. It smelled like fig, raw hamburger meat, and Luci.

The scent was probably left over from when she

went to meet the Egg Man the day before. Her scent had a way of lingering for days. I knew from experience.

Drinking rice wine in my apartment, I pondered what the next week's painting would be. There was a half-dead fetus fly and a woman giving birth to fetus flies.

I thought maybe the next one should have something to do with Luci but also have something to do with fetus flies. It should have something to do with the human life cycle. I did the birth and death of fetus flies.

I wanted to do something sexual and gritty.

Using the memory method, I was able to figure out a decent idea. I would paint Luci and I making love in Luci's scummy apartment. I could give Luci wings. There was something poetic and natural about the nude body with wings. People don't like to think of themselves as grown up versions of fetus flies so they pretend like they weren't supposed to have wings. We are winged creatures, though, even though we've forgotten how to fly.

I thought if I did it right, the painting would be emotionally raw. It would be sexual, primal, filthy, and *real*. It would go well with my other two smell paintings and it would be a lot of fun painting Luci again.

While I was contemplating the painting, I heard the gur-gling/rumbling noises of the Egg Man next door as I often did. Then I heard a different noise coming from the wall. It was a thumping noise.

I pressed my ear against the west wall and I heard moaning. I heard a woman shouting and whining. It sounded like Luci.

I went to apartment 314. The door was unlocked. Inside, I saw Luci on top of the Egg Man. She was naked, strad-dling his enormous egg-shaped brain. Her legs were around the Egg Man's shoulders. His face was buried in her crotch. She was forcing the mutant to give her oral sex while she tongued his brain. Her body covered only a quarter of his head as she lay atop it. She rubbed her breasts and arms against him. His smells were mixing with her smells.

Luci saw me in the doorway. She turned and stared at me. She licked the Egg Man's brain at me seductively.

I'm trying to suck out the souls she said.

The Egg Man's moans were muffled in Luci's crotch. It was as if he was getting sexual pleasure from having Luci rub herself on his great blob of a head. I could only see his chin fat and a squirreling gray tongue beneath Luci's ass.

Luci just stared at me, rubbing her cheek into the brain like a squishy pillow.

The sexual stimulation of the Egg Man's brain seemed to be intensifying the odor in the room. I suddenly felt nauseous and tumbled out of the doorway. I ran back to my apartment and chugged rice wine to keep the vomit down.

Luci came in a couple hours later and grabbed the rice wine from my hand. She took a swig and sat on my bed. She acted as if nothing had happened. She smelled like fig and raw hamburger meat.

She said how'd they like your painting?

I took my bottle back from Luci but the rim was covered in Egg Man juice so I put it off to the side.

They loved it I said.

She said are you going to paint another one?

Yeah I said.

You should paint me fucking the Egg Man she said.

A chill went up my spine.

That would be intense she said.

I said I don't know.

She said there's something deeply sexual about those mega-brains. I want to know what it's like to have one. Did you know that anyone could get an implant from Heaven Inc. if they pass the compatibility test?

I plugged my nose at her.

She said you have to have a special kind of brain for it to work. You have to have a strong imagination. I'm sure if we went in we'd both pass the test.

I said you should get out of here. The OSM workers will get back here any minute.

She said what are you scared of big bald Tony or something?

He threatened to kill me I said.

She said Tony's a Feel so he's a wimp. Hit him lightly in the stomach and he'll run away crying.

I still think you should go I said.

No she said.

I said no?

She said no. I'm not going to leave. You're not going to kick me out.

I clenched a fist. I wanted to pick her up and throw her smelly ass out of the room.

I'll see you tomorrow I said.

She said maybe I have plans tomorrow. I want to stay here and discuss our next painting.

Our next painting?

I think you should paint me fucking the Egg Man she said.

I said I kind of have another idea already.

She said fuck the other idea.

I don't want to paint the Egg Man I said.

She said why not?

I said because he's disgusting.

She said then it will be a more powerful painting.

She came over to me.

She said if you don't do what I want I'm going to fuck you with Egg Man juice all over me.

I pushed her away from me.

She forced herself closer and pulled off my pants.

I don't want to I said.

She took off her clothes and pressed her body up against my face. She smelled of fig, raw hamburger meat, ammonia, rotten bell peppers, dead earwigs, and water chestnuts, all mixed together with menstrual blood. I didn't notice it before but I could now tell that Luci was on her period. I could smell it. It was strong and overwhelming. I gagged at the thought of the Egg Man giving her oral sex while she was menstruating.

She said I'm not going to stop until you do what I want.

She slid me inside of her and then fucked me.

The smell of the Egg Man and her period engulfed me, made me dizzy.

I said okay I'll do it just get the fuck away from me.

No, it's too late she said.

And she continued fucking.

She wiped a finger across my face. The finger smelled like Egg Man cum, hot shit, and dead animals. I pulled my face away and puked down the side of the bed.

And she continued fucking.

The next morning, Luci posed for me on top of the Egg Man's head. She had her crotch in the Egg Man's face again. Her menstrual blood was trickling against his lips.

He's a Taste Luci said.

I cringed.

She said but he's not a wimp like you.

I watched as the Egg Man lapped up Luci's blood. For a Taste, it should have been a living hell, but it was as if he was only giving her oral sex because he actually liked the taste of it.

This is too obscene for me I said.

Just paint it Luci said.

I'm creating art not pornography I said.

Sex is art she said.

It can't be trashy I said.

She said why the hell not?

I spent the next few days painting Luci and the Egg Man. I collected their smells into my paint as they wiggled against each other.

Don't forget the blood Luci said.

She lifted her leg so that I could swab some out of her vagina with my paint brush.

The smells of the Egg Man were complex and difficult to get right. I couldn't just use the smell of his sweat. I had to collect the smell of the grease and exhaust from the machines around him.

It was a long project. It required a lot more work than my previous painting. I wished I would have done the other painting instead.

Once it was finally finished I didn't bother showing Luci or the Egg Man. I took it out of the room and left them to their depraved carnalities. I didn't want anything to do with them. They probably didn't even notice that I had gone.

I showed the Egg Man painting to the review board at the end of the week. They thought it was disgusting and amazing. They wanted me to do three more just like it.

Chapter #10

A couple of days passed and I hadn't seen Luci. Every once in a while I would hear her through the wall fucking the Egg Man.

Fucking bitch I would say to the wall.

I was trying to do another painting in my room, but I didn't have any inspiration. I thought of doing one where a teenaged girl was giving birth to fetus flies and feeding them to an aquarium filled with frogs. I thought of doing a self portrait of myself lying naked on my bed in this dumpy apartment. I thought of stabbing myself in the face with the hunting knife that Squik had given me.

I thought that drinking PBR was much better than thinking.

There was a knock at the door. I opened it to a large gray blur that slammed me to the floor.

I told you not to fuck my bitch no more said the intruder.

He had a strong OSM accent.

From the ground, I looked up. It was Tony, the bald-head OSM worker.

He shut the door behind him and pulled out a pocket knife.

He said now I'm going to have to cut you up so that she won't want to fuck you anymore.

I remembered what Luci had said. He was a Feel. That meant pain was more intense to him. He would be easy to hurt.

I grabbed an empty bottle of rice wine and hit the OSM with it as hard as I could in the shin. The bottle didn't break, but he screamed out and fell backwards.

Fuck, fuck, fuck he cried.

While he was down, I hit him in the head with the bottle and it broke in half. He shrieked and kicked me in the stomach as hard as he could. Then he charged me.

I then realized that although Feels were more susceptible to pain, they were also more susceptible to bursts of adrenalin caused by pain. By breaking the bottle of rice wine over the OSM's head, I had only made him stronger and angrier.

Now I'm going to have to kill you he said.

He swung his stubby knife at me but I ducked out of the way. He only scratched me a bit on the arm. I jumped behind my blank canvas and pushed it at him. He smacked the canvas with his knife arm, causing the knife to puncture the fabric. The blade was caught on the frame.

While his weapon was stuck I looked for the hunting knife that Squik had given me. It was on the floor near the toilet.

Tony got his knife out of the canvas and lunged at me just as I was lurching for the toilet. He tripped on the canvas and fell on the floor next to me.

I seized the hunting knife and brought it towards him. We stabbed each other at the same time. We were in awkward positions, so the blades went into our flesh slowly.

His knife wasn't very sharp. It cut into my shoulder but he couldn't get it in very far. It stopped at the bone. My hunting knife dug deep into his belly one inch at a time.

We were just lying there facing each other for a while, our knives inside of each other. His expression was one of shock. I felt his flesh quivering through my knife. The pain was so overwhelming for him that he couldn't say or do anything anymore.

It took him twenty minutes to die. He didn't say a word during that time. We just watched each other. Neither of us let go of our knives.

In the last five minutes he cried quietly to himself.

I wanted to say something to him, to comfort him, but I had a knife inside of his gut.

After he was dead, I said she's not your bitch she's my bitch.

I sat quietly in the room with the body for a while. Then I cleaned my wound, drank a PBR, and ate a bag of potato chips. I didn't know what I was going to do. I wasn't the killing type.

If he threatens you again you kill him before he kills you Squik had said. You need to be a survivor. You need to be able to defend yourself.

Squik's words rang through my head.

I thought am I a survivor?

I paced back and forth, drinking my beer, staring at Tony. I had to come up with a way to get rid of the body. If anybody in the building saw this I would be dead. His friends would avenge him.

After watching the body for nearly an hour, I realized something. I realized that this view was almost poetic. The way Tony's corpse wrapped itself around my antique toilet with his ragged OSM uniform, his freshly shaven head, and my hunting knife buried deep inside of his stomach; it was a heart-wrenching sight. It was depressing. He had died such a pointless, pathetic death. He died over Luci. He died over a worthless smelly whore, a woman who didn't care about him, a woman who didn't care about anybody but herself. It was the death of a working class fool. It would make a great painting.

I thought after I get rid of the body I might have to paint this scene.

Then I thought but how am I going to capture these smells? How am I going to get the smell of Tony's sweat, his blood, his OSM uniform?

I have to paint it right now I said to myself.

So I got to work.

I sketched Tony's corpse and then painted him. I acted quickly while his smells were still fresh. I scraped the odors from his body in the way that I had done with Luci. Then I pulled the odors out of the toilet, the floor, the sink. I collected the mold growing on the wall behind the toilet. I scraped rust from the metal of the hunting knife and rubber from the handle of the knife.

I'm a survivor I said to the corpse, as I chugged another PBR and tossed the can across the room.

If you try to kill me I will kill you I said, smiling through a drunken daze.

The painting was proof that I had killed the man. If anybody saw it they would know I had done the deed. This piece was putting my life in danger. I could die because of this piece.

But it was art. I was born to die for my art.

I was covered in blood and paint when I went to Squik's room. I told him what had happened.

You fucked up Squik said when he saw Tony's body.

The fear in his voice surprised me. I was expecting him to be more understanding of my actions.

I said I thought you said this is what I should do?

Squik said but OSM has a police force. Their job is to kill anyone who murders their workers.

I said it was in self defense. It was his fault.

Squik said he was trying to kill a competitor for his mate. That's what men are supposed to do. He was just acting upon his instincts. You were the one in the wrong.

I said I was just trying to live. You said I need to be a survivor.

He said killing an OSM on their territory isn't good for survival.

I said what am I going to do?

He said we need to get rid of the body as soon as possible.

We dumped the body in the alley behind the Henry Building. Squik said that as long as his body wasn't in my apartment I would be fine.

After we buried his body in a pile of trash, I looked up to see if anyone had seen us. There was a woman staring down from the fifth floor. She was wearing a gray jumpsuit. It looked like an OSM uniform.

Oh shit Squik said.

He took off and I followed.

Back in his room, Squik freaked out.

He said the OSM cops are going to find out for sure now, man. Even if they are too busy with the war to deal with you, the other OSM residents of this building are going to come after you without mercy.

He gave me a gun.

He said do you have a place far away from here that you can move to?

I said I might be able to ask the GO for a new apartment next week.

He said stay with Luci until then and whatever you do don't show your face in the halls unless the OSMs are at the mill.

I agreed and he pushed me out of his apartment as hard as he could.

I knocked on Luci's door.

She didn't answer.

It was unlocked so I went inside and closed the door.

My jaw went slack when I saw it. She was on her mattress, masturbating, holding it up with her left hand and licking her fingers.

Her brain was seven feet high. She had gotten an implant from Heaven Inc. She shaved her head and turned herself into a mega-brain just like the Egg Man.

Her brain was much smaller than the Egg Man's. It was new so it wasn't yet swollen with information. It was a long beehive-shaped shaft. It looked like she had a brain-textured dick growing out of her skull.

She said am I beautiful?

She caressed the shaft of her brain, digging her fingers beneath her legs.

I can feel the souls inside of me she said, moaning.

I backed away from her.

She said I am like their god.

I turned around and left the room. As I crossed the hallway I could hear her cry out as she reached orgasm.

My face was red and trembling as I paced in my N-shaped apartment, brooding, kicking beer cans across the floor.

I said what the fuck did she do to herself?

My voice was loud. I wanted her to be able to hear me.

You made yourself into a freak I said.

I thought is she in love with the Egg Man now? Did she love him so much that she wanted to be like him? She is so disgusting. She is more disgusting than ever. She ruined herself. I don't want to have anything to do with her anymore. It's over between us. She's dead to me.

I held the gun with both hands and kept it pointed at the doorway. If any of Tony's friends knew where I lived I planned to shoot them before they could shoot me.

I thought if that girl that saw us really was OSM

and she recognized Squik, then they would go after him first. But if confronted and threatened Squik might tell them I was the one who killed Tony. He might tell them where I live.

Then I thought they might go after Luci. Tony's friends probably know all about Luci. They probably know how overbearing and jealous he was when it came to her. They probably know she was sleeping around with a lot of people. They might assume that she had something to do with his death. They might think she manipulated some new boyfriend into killing Tony for her, to get him off her back.

I decided that I had to warn Luci. She was in danger.

I made sure nobody was in the hallway when I snuck into Luci's apartment. She was still masturbating and caressing her mega-brain.

Luci I said.

Yes she said.

She stared at me with her mouth open, licking her lips at me.

I stuttered. I didn't tell her what had happened. I couldn't. How was I supposed to tell her that OSM people might be out to get her without telling her about what had happened to Tony? I couldn't tell her about Tony. She might have had feelings for him. She might have thought of me as a monster for killing him. Or, even worse, she might have turned me in to the OSMs to save her own butt.

So I just stood there in the center of her messy room, watching her masturbate. She watched me back, but she didn't say anything.

Then I noticed the smell. Her brain was sweating a thick juice that filled the room with a powerful odor. But it didn't smell like the Egg Man's odor. It didn't smell of fig, raw hamburger meat, ammonia, rotten bell peppers, dead earwigs, and water chestnuts. It smelled just as complex, but much more pleasing. Much, *much* more pleasing.

It smelled of orange blossoms, dates, salted almonds, white wine, sweet meats, and buttered lobster.

Her pulsing fleshy brain looked so disgusting, yet smelled so delicious that it drew me closer to her. I had to inhale the scent deeper.

Luci had said that body odor was designed to be an aphrodisiac. I didn't believe her. Something so repulsive could never turn me on. However, this strange smell emanating from Luci's big disgusting brain was somehow turning me on.

I closed my eyes and breathed deeply through my nostrils.

As a Smell, I had never sensed anything so sexual. I have seen erotic images, I have felt erotic sensations, but I have never before smelled erotic scents. Luci's new smell was like smelling sex.

I could feel my penis growing in my pants, as I leaned in close to Luci and smelled her erect brain. Her body still reeked of its usual rancid filth, but the brain juice was strong enough to overpower it.

It's so sexy I said.

My words made her moan with pleasure.

I said it smells so beautiful. It's really turning me on.

Her eyes were closed. She caressed her brain quickly now, like her brain was one giant dick that she was masturbating.

Let me fuck you I said.

She licked her lips.

I started to take off my clothes.
No she said.
I said what?
I don't want you to fuck me she said.
I said why not?
She said I want you to paint me.

Although it was empty at the time, I forgot to check the hallway for OSMs before crossing to collect my art supplies. I also forgot to bring the gun with me on my way back to Luci's.

I knew this was reckless behavior on my part. If the OSMs found me in Luci's apartment we would both be dead, but I was so aroused by Luci's new smell that I couldn't control myself. I couldn't think clearly.

She didn't stop masturbating the entire time I painted her, having orgasm after orgasm. Her eyes were closed. For all I knew, she could have been making love with all of the souls within her brain.

She didn't let me have sex with her, but I decided I didn't need to have sex with her. Just smelling her was pleasure enough. It was even *better* than sex.

I collected smells from her surroundings first: her sweat-stained mattress, her crusty sheets, her mold-caked wall. Then I collected the smells from her skin. Starting with the unpleasant smells, to get them out of the way. She let me touch her labia briefly so that I could collect some moisture for when I painted her vagina.

After I had painted her body and the background, I started on the brain. I saved the best for last. Getting the smell of her brain juice on my fingers was a sensual experience in itself. I brought the flavor to my nostrils and inhaled deeply. The scent made my eyes role back, my muscles loosen, and my mind drift in drunken ecstasy.

I wanted to lick the picture of the brain as I painted it. I wanted to consume it and make it a part of me. Though I didn't technically have sex, it was the best sex I ever had. Though I didn't have an orgasm, the experience was like one long unending orgasm.

Luci fell asleep before I finished the painting. She had climaxed so many times that she had forgotten that I was there. She slept with a smile on her face, as if she was still basking in the warm after-sex glow.

The painting was the most sensual work I had ever created. It did not have the dramatic power of my two previous paintings, but it did have power.

I wasn't sure if it was safe to leave Luci alone that night, but I decided to go back to my apartment. The worst thing would be for the OSMs to find the two of us together.

I was in my bed with the gun on my chest. I couldn't sleep. I couldn't stop thinking. My thoughts flipped between the panic of being hunted by OSMs and the excitement about Luci's mega-brain. I also wondered if Luci liked me again. I wondered if she would be my girlfriend. I wondered if she would be willing to get serious.

Whatever the case, I knew I wanted to be with her. I could put up with the ugliness of her brain, the stink of her body odor, her filth, her rudeness, her laziness, as long as I could be with her.

I stared at the painting of Luci's mega-brain propped up on my shelf. I could smell it from all the way across the room. I had captured the experience perfectly. I couldn't wait for the morning to come, so that I could show Luci how great it turned out.

In the middle of the night, I awoke to the sound of Luci moaning through my wall. She was next door, fucking the Egg Man. I jumped out of bed and listened carefully. It was her. She was screaming with pleasure.

I said what the fuck? You fucking bitch.

I couldn't believe she would go see the Egg Man after what we had shared earlier that night. I couldn't believe she would do that to me.

I thought why didn't she come to my apartment? She should want to see my new painting of her. She hasn't seen it yet. I figured that was the first thing she would want to do after she woke up.

My eyes watered up. I buried my head in my pillow clenched my jaw as tight as I could until my ears were ringing.

She wanted to be an egghead and fuck other eggheads?

Fuck her I said.

Tony's smell was still in the room. His blood was still on my floor. When I closed my eyes, it was like his body was still lying there, haunting me. I looked at the painting of him. It was the best painting I had ever created. Better than the painting of Luci masturbating. It smelled so real. It was as if I literally captured Tony's soul when I painted it. After he died, I had taken his soul out of his body and mixed it into the paint.

Within the picture, I could smell the sadness and frustration that Tony had felt as he died. I could smell the anger, the betrayal. I could smell his longing for Luci and his . . . hatred of Luci. The smell wasn't noticeable before, but the more I sniffed the clearer it became. The smell told me that Tony hated Luci.

As a Feel, Tony must have been disturbed by her filth. Whenever she pressed her body against him, she must have made him feel itchy, slimy, sticky, and dirty. She probably tormented him in the same way that she tormented me.

Tony had more in common with me than I had thought.

Squik had said that Tony had the right to kill me because I was a competitor for his mate. The Egg Man was also a competitor. He was my competition. He was in my way. He was ruining things for me. I wondered if I had the right to kill him.

The next day, I just stayed in my apartment, hiding out. I was expecting OSMs to bust in at any moment, but they never came. Luci didn't come to my door, either. I didn't want to go to her door. If she would have come to me I might have forgiven her.

She was probably in danger, but I didn't care. The OSMs could go ahead and kill her. I was done being jerked around.

After the sun went down, there was a commotion in the hallway. A lot of yelling in other languages. I didn't know what was going on. I just sat in my bed with the gun in my hand, waiting.

Eventually, I couldn't take it any more. I had to see Luci. I had to make sure she was alright.

There was nobody in the hallway when I opened the

door, so I left the gun on my bed. I didn't want to have to explain to Luci why I was carrying a gun.

Luci's door was already open a crack, so I let myself in. She wasn't there. I went into my apartment and listened at my west wall. The Egg Man and Luci weren't having sex in there. I listened carefully. I didn't hear anybody's voice.

I went into the hallway and smelled the door to room 314. I couldn't find her scent.

I entered the Egg Man's apartment.

The Egg Man was alone. He watched me with his tiny yellow eyes as I entered.

I said where is she?

Gone he said.

I said where did she go?

He said I don't know.

Slime dripped down his brain onto his face.

I said I heard you fucking last night.

Nope he said.

She's my bitch I said.

My voice sounded like Tony's.

He said she doesn't want me anymore. She has her own mega-brain now. I've lost my appeal.

I should kill you I said.

I stood over him. He was helpless in his condition. This was the man who was taking Luci away from me? I could cut his jugular with my hunting knife and he couldn't do anything about it. I could shoot him. I could strangle him with his own feeding tube and everybody would think it was an accident.

He saw me looking at the feeding tube.

It wouldn't be wise to try to kill me gurgled the Egg Man.

I said why not?

Heaven Inc. is a powerful company. It is small but they have allegiances with every major corporation out there. Nobody kills a Heaven brain and gets away with it.

I kneeled into his stomach and wrapped his feeding tube around his throat, then tightened.

I said not if I make it look like an accident.

Squeezing tighter, he began to wheeze. Egg Man juice was getting all over my clothes.

He said you can't . . .

I choked him until his mammoth brain turned red. He slid a hand beneath the feeding tube and loosened its hold around his throat so that he could speak.

He said there are hundreds of thousands of souls in my brain. If you kill me they all die. What gives you the right to kill all of those people?

I said this is the survival of the fittest. If they can't defend themselves then they deserve to die.

The feeding tube crushed his throat.

He said please . . .

I pulled tighter, so tight that my knuckles turned purple. Then he went limp.

Looking at the Egg Man's dead body, I decided that I had to paint him. A dead egg head would make a powerful painting. I thought it was a shame that I had to kill him, but at least he will live forever in the shape of a painting.

I was saturated with the smell of fig and raw hamburger as I entered the hallway to retrieve my painting supplies. While wiping the Egg Man juice off of my clothes, I didn't notice the people coming towards me.

The OSM girl who had seen Squik and I dump the body was heading my way with three large men. It was like they were on patrol, two of them carrying baseball bats and one of them carrying a rifle.

She said there he is.

The OSM with the rifle aimed at me and fired. The

bullet hit me in the ear. It went straight through the lobe and grazed the side of my head. I could smell droplets of my blood splattered on the wall behind me.

I ducked down and ran for the western stairwell.

Get him said the woman.

He charged down the stairs, firing his gun. The others yelled and slammed their bats against the walls as they thundered after me. I had left my gun in my apartment. It was too late to fight back.

All I could do was flee.

Chapter #12

I ran out of the front entrance of the Henry Building into the street, the OSMs still a floor or two behind me. My ear was splashing blood all over the steps.

I wished Squik was with me to back me up. I wished I wouldn't have left my gun in the apartment.

In the street, I was greeted by twenty men holding shotguns. They pointed them at me. That was it. I was caught. I stopped running and held up my hands. Blood squirted out of the side of my head as I told them that it wasn't my fault.

It was self defense I said.

Then I realized something. These men were wearing red jumpsuits. They weren't OSMs they were MSMs. They were there for war.

I dropped to the ground as the male OSMs exited the building behind me. Their mouths dropped open at the sight of all the red uniforms. Before they could react, the MSMs sprayed them with shotgun blasts. Their blood splattered across pavement.

I got up and ran back into the building as the MSMs

made sure the two gray-suits were dead. I passed the OSM woman and charged up the stairs. She screamed at me and tried punching me as I passed. Then a shotgun blast knocked her off her feet and slammed her against a mass of her own blood on the wall behind her.

Upstairs, I went into my room to grab my gun. I heard shotgun fire downstairs. A *lot* of shotgun fire. The war had begun.

OSMs and other residents ran up and down the hallway.

The OSMs cried get higher, get higher.

The other residents just cried.

I ran down the hallway to Squik's apartment. His door was wide open. His place had been trashed. He wasn't there. I stepped inside. Squik's kid, Gordi was there. He was crumbled into a ball in the corner. His head had been taken off.

The OSMs must have done this. They must have taken Squik and killed his kid.

I wondered if they had taken Luci as well. I wondered if she was already dead.

She's in danger I said to the decapitated child.

I had to save her.

The MSMs were going room to room, floor to floor, shooting the residents of the Henry Building in their beds. It was a clean sweep.

My survival instinct kicked in. I had to go higher.

I went out in the hall and pointed my gun at one of the Toyota girls who was standing in a panic in the hallway.

She screamed something Toyotan and I lowered the gun. She followed me down the hallway.

Get out of here I said.

She waved her hands around and babbled some gibberish. She didn't speak common.

I saw a handful of red-suits come up the west stairwell, so I turned to run for the east stairwell. But OSMs were coming down the east stairwell with handguns and rifles to meet their rivals on the third floor. There were going to collide on this floor and I was stuck in the middle.

The Toyotan followed me as I ran back to my apartment, but she didn't follow me inside.

Come on I said.

She didn't understand.

When the shooting started, I watched as the Toyota woman was cut to pieces in the crossfire.

I looked out of my window. Several more MSMs were in the street with flamethrowers. They were setting the building on fire.

Fuck I said.

I had to protect my paintings. The review board kept all of the pieces I brought them, so the only paintings I had to worry about saving were the one of Tony and the one of Luci. I cut them out of their frames and rolled them up into a tube. I had to get them to safety.

I grabbed my duffle bag from under my bed, the one that contained all of my possessions in the world. There was extra room in the bag, so I filled it up with as many painting supplies as I could. As I hysterically packed my brushes and papers, I heard gurgling and bubbling noises coming from the west wall. They sounded like noises the Egg Man used to make.

I shook it off. The Egg Man was dead. I was just hearing things. With all the gunfire it was impossible to hear anything clearly.

With a mirror, I peaked outside of my doorway to see how many of them were still in the hall. Five OSMs had fallen, only two remained. There were still eight red-suits.

I watched with the mirror until the two OSMs retreated back into the stairwell. The MSMs didn't chase after them. They continued breaking into the apartments one-by-one to shoot the occupants within.

My survival instinct told me that this was my only chance to make a move. I jumped into the hallway and fired my handgun at the MSMs. I ran backwards toward the east stairwell as I went. Not a single one of my bullets hit a target, but they distracted them enough that they couldn't get any good shots off at me.

I made it thirty feet down the hallway without getting shot, but then I tripped over a dead OSM and fell to the ground. And worse than that, I was out of bullets.

The red-suits came at me. I tried looking for a gun on the dead OSM but he didn't seem to have one. I raised my

153

hands at them and tried to tell them that I wasn't OSM. They didn't care.

Something stopped them in their tracks. There was a rumbling sound. The building was shaking. The red-suits looked around, confused about what was happening.

A wall exploded open and a mammoth crashed into the hallway, knocking two of the red suits to the ground. The thing roared and gurgled. It turned around and looked at me. It was the Egg Man. He wasn't dead. I hadn't killed him. I had just pissed him off.

He glared at me with mad yellow eyes. There didn't seem to be any life behind them.

The Egg Man moved forward, pulling his enormous brain behind him. The walls cracked and crumbled around the brain as he pulled his way through.

The red-suits fired at the Egg Man from behind and he cried out. He roared like a crazed elephant and turned around to face his attackers. They hit him five times at pointblank range. The shotgun blasts only made him more angry.

I got up and ran towards the eastern stairwell. Looking back, the Egg Man was stomping on one of the MSM's skulls, crushing the man's tiny brain out of his head.

There was gunfire at the bottom of the stairwell. The two surviving OSMs from the third floor gunfight had gone downstairs and gotten themselves into another stand off.

My survival instinct took me upstairs.

I found Squik and Luci on the fifth floor. They were tied up in an abandoned apartment. Squik had a bullet in his chest. Luci wasn't moving either. Her giant tube-shaped brain was propped up against the wall behind her.

Nobody else was on the fifth floor.

I looked out of the window. The first two floors were on fire. It wouldn't be long before the third was aflame. The people who ran out of the building to escape the flames were shot down by the MSMs in the street.

I caressed Luci's cheek until she woke up.

She said what's going on?

I sniffed deeply at her brain slime as I untied her.

The MSMs are attacking I said.

She looked out of the window.

They're killing everyone I said.

She stood up and held her long brain with both hands.

She said what are we going to do?

Fly I said.

I took off my clothes.

She said fly?

I buzzed my dragonfly wings at her.

You can't really fly with those she said.

I said my wings aren't strong enough to lift us off the ground, but I think they're strong enough to give us a slow fall.

There was a loud roaring sound and the floor rumbled beneath our feet.

Luci said what was that?

I said it's the Egg Man. He's fighting the MSMs.

We have to go help him she said.

He's not going to make it I said.

She went towards the door. I grabbed her by the arm.

I said come on, forget him.

She said I'm not leaving without him.

He's going to die I said.

Then I'll die with him she said.

I said I love you, Luci.

I don't care she said.

I tightened my grip on Luci's arm.

I said what are you doing? You can't be in love with the Egg Man. You're a leech. You don't love anyone but yourself.

She pulled her arm out of my grip.

You don't know anything about me she said.

Fuck you I said.

When she turned to leave, I grabbed a lamp off of the table and hit her in her giant ugly brain. Her head jerked hard and I heard a loud crack.

Her neck broke under the weight of her head. Her body went limp and fell into my arms.

I turned her over and held her giant wrinkled head in my lap. I started to cry.

I'm sorry I said, as I caressed her brain.

The screams of the Egg Man filled the apartment building as the fire took the third floor.

I cried and pounded on Luci's sweaty chest.

I said why didn't you want to come with me? I could have saved you. We could have moved into a beautiful uptown apartment together. I would have painted, you would have been my inspiration. Now you're dead.

I pushed her corpse off of me. Her head hit the floor with a thump. I wiped the tears from my eyes.

I have to paint you I said to Luci. I have to capture

your soul in a painting.

I picked her off of the floor and draped her over my shoulder. With her giant brain dragging behind, I carried her up the stairwell all the way to the roof. I had to climb as high as possible so that I would have the maximum amount of time to paint her before the building was consumed by flames. Once outside, I closed the door behind me and barred it so that nobody could disturb my work.

I was going to paint the picture I originally wanted. The one where Luci and I were making love. Only instead of both of us having wings, I would be the one with the wings and she would have the long mega-brain. It was what she would have wanted.

Taking the art supplies out of my duffle bag, I realized that I didn't have all of the colors I needed. I had red, white, a light brown, and a dark brown. I decided to just use these colors. The smell was what was important.

I stripped Luci naked and propped her up in a corner of the roof. I wrapped my body around her, positioning myself where I would be if we were having sex. Although I had always been on the bottom, in this image I was going to put myself on top. I wanted my back to be showing so that I could make the wings more prominent in the painting.

I removed a piece of loose canvas paper from my duffel bag. Then I sketched Luci's image quickly, and what I imagined my image looked like on top of her. Halfway through the sketch, the pencil broke. I didn't have time to sharpen it so I tossed it away and went straight to the painting. I collected Luci's smells and mixed them into the paints, using a roof shingle as a palette. I pulled her essence out of her skin, out of her brain, and mixed them into the paint. I even collected the souls within her megabrain for when I painted her head.

As I painted, I was filled with raw artistic power. Every stroke was perfect. Every smell rubbed on in just the right way. I was high on the smell of Luci's brain juice. I was filled with adrenalin and sexual energy. Luci was coming to life again, in my work.

As I painted, I forgot that I was holding a brush. I forgot that I was on top of a burning building. I felt as if I had become a part of the painting. I was inside of it, having sex with Luci right there on the rooftop. She was tormenting me with her stink and I was loving every minute of it. There was no Egg Man, or Tony, or Squik to come between us. There was only a deep primal lust.

I was too engulfed in my work to do anything about the people in the stairwell. They banged on the door to the roof, crying for somebody to let them out. I didn't help them. I didn't want them to ruin my moment.

By the time I had finished the painting, the banging had already stopped. Flames had engulfed the building all the way to the top floor.

I admired my work of art. It was flawless. A masterpiece. Luci's soul and her delicious brain smell had been preserved perfectly in the picture. I even captured the smell of the smoke as the building burned.

The painting would have gotten messed up if I rolled it, so I carried it open. I collected my other two paintings and held them close to my heart.

As I stepped up onto the edge of the roof, I allowed the wind to blow against my naked body. I peered down at the red soldiers below. They were killing the last of the OSMs.

I looked over at Luci's body. At first, I was going to kiss it goodbye, but then I realized that the body was just an empty shell. The real Luci was coming with me, within the painting in my hands.

I flapped my dragonfly wings and jumped.

It was a surprising sensation. The wings weren't weak. They turned out to be strong. I flew off of the Henry Building into the air. They worked. They must have always worked.

I sailed over the MSMs across the street like a dragonfly. The MSMs were so far down they looked tiny. They were just ants to me. They didn't have minds of their own. They just did their queen's bidding. I wasn't an ant. I was an artist.

I was free.

Bullets tore through my wings and back. I spun out of control. A shotgun blast shredded my legs. Another ripped through the left side of my body. I went down. From high up in the sky, I fell far.

I splattered against the pavement. I lay there, paralyzed in a pile of my own guts, watching as red ants marched two-by-two towards me.

As my vision faded, I noticed that my masterpiece was still mostly intact. It was going to be okay even if I was not.

I could smell Luci lying next to me within the canvas. It made me feel good to be next to her as my consciousness drifted away. But then I realized that she wasn't trying to comfort me with her stink. It smelled like she was laughing at me.

Epilogue

I wasn't dead yet. I was in the GO hospital, lying in a bed, pumped full of drugs. Pieces of my body were missing. I lost a leg and my left arm. I couldn't move my right arm. My lips had been torn off. I was a wreck.

The bearded man from the GO review board was in the room with me. He approached my bed.

He said are you awake, Lincoln?

I nodded.

Good he said.

He cleared his throat and straightened his tie. He still never bothered to introduce himself.

He said there was extensive nerve damage to your arms. They had to amputate your left arm and the right side of your body has become paralyzed. Your left leg is missing, we're not sure what happened to it.

I tried to move my right arm and leg. He was right. They didn't work.

I said what about my paintings? Did you save my paintings?

He said the ones that were with you when you were

brought in? They are a little damaged but I believe they are salvageable.

Thank you I said.

It would have been terrible if my paintings were lost. That would have meant that all I went through was for nothing.

The bearded man said it saddens me to say this but you'll never be able to paint again. We have no choice but to revoke your grant.

I said but what about my work? I have a ground-breaking style.

He said believe me, many on the board were really pulling for you. But we're going to have to cut our losses and walk away. Your work will not go to waste, though. The committee has discussed it and we are going to put another artist's name on your paintings. This new artist, who is a Smell, will take over where you left off.

I said but I painted them . . .

My eyes wanted to tear but they were all dried up.

He said I'm sorry, but you know as well as I that this is the way the art world works.

The bearded man waved two nurses over to my hospital bed.

He said if you like they can give you a lethal injection. I think that would be the most humane thing to do for you in your current state.

I said what? No, I want to live.

The bearded man said do you understand what has happened to you? You are paralyzed on one side of your body and you are missing the arm and leg of the other side. You are completely invalid.

I said I don't care. I want to live.

My survival instinct wasn't going to let them just kill me then and there. I was a survivor. I was one of the strong.

The bearded man cupped his hands together.

Well take him outside I guess he said to the nurses.

The nurses wheeled my bed towards the door.

I said wait, what are you doing?

The bearded man said you are no longer a citizen of the GO, which means that you won't have use of the hospital facilities anymore.

I said what am I going to do? How am I going to survive out there?

Through the kindness of strangers said the bearded man.

The nurses wheeled me outside and dropped me on the steps outside of the GO building. I tried to move, but nothing worked, only my mouth.

Over the next few days, I asked for help from the people walking up and down the steps. None of them even looked at me. They were busy with their own lives, their own survival.

By the next day the sun had bleached the color out of my eyes, my skin was burnt, my flesh had turned to rot, and an army of black ants were beginning to eat me alive.

ABOUT THE AUTHOR

Carlton Mellick III is one of the leading authors in the new *Bizarro* genre uprising. In only a few short years, his surreal counterculture novels have drawn an international cult following despite the fact that they have been shunned by most libraries and corporate bookstores. He lives in Portland, OR, where Pabst Blue Ribbon is the major form of currency.

Visit him online at **www.avantpunk.com**

Bizarro books

CATALOGUE – SPRING 200

Bizarro Books publishes under the following imprints:

www.rawdogscreamingpress.com

www.eraserheadpress.co

www.afterbirthbooks.com

www.swallowdownpress.co

For all your Bizarro needs visit:

WWW.BIZARROCENTRAL.COM

Introduce yourselves to the bizarro genre and all of its authors with the *Bizarro Starter Kit* series. Each volume features short novels and short stories by ten of the leading bizarro authors, designed to give you a perfect sampling of the genre for only $5 plus shipping.

BB-0X1
"The Bizarro Starter Kit"
(Orange)

Featuring D. Harlan Wilson, Carlton Mellick III, Jeremy Robert Johnson, Kevin L Donihe, Gina Ranalli, Andre Duza, Vincent W. Sakowski, Steve Beard, John Edward Lawson, and Bruce Taylor.

236 pages $5

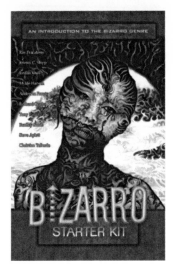

BB-0X2
"The Bizarro Starter Kit"
(Blue)

Featuring Ray Fracalossy, Jeremy C. Shipp, Jordan Krall, Mykle Hansen, Andersen Prunty, Eckhard Gerdes, Bradley Sands, Steve Aylett, Christian TeBordo, and Tony Rauch.

244 pages $5

BB-001 "The Kafka Effekt" D. Harlan Wilson - A collection of forty-four irreal short stories loosely written in the vein of Franz Kafka, with more than a pinch of William S. Burroughs sprinkled on top. **211 pages $14**

BB-002 "Satan Burger" Carlton Mellick III - The cult novel that put Carlton Mellick III on the map ... Six punks get jobs at a fast food restaurant owned by the devil in a city violently overpopulated by surreal alien cultures. **236 pages $14**

BB-003 "Some Things Are Better Left Unplugged" Vincent Sakwoski - Join The Man and his Nemesis, the obese tabby, for a nightmare roller coaster ride into this postmodern fantasy. **152 pages $10**

BB-004 "Shall We Gather At the Garden?" Kevin L Donihe - Donihe's Debut novel. Midgets take over the world, The Church of Lionel Richie vs. The Church of the Byrds, plant porn and more! **244 pages $14**

BB-005 "Razor Wire Pubic Hair" Carlton Mellick III - A genderless humandildo is purchased by a razor dominatrix and brought into her nightmarish world of bizarre sex and mutilation. **176 pages $11**

BB-006 "Stranger on the Loose" D. Harlan Wilson - The fiction of Wilson's 2nd collection is planted in the soil of normalcy, but what grows out of that soil is a dark, witty, otherworldly jungle... **228 pages $14**

BB-007 "The Baby Jesus Butt Plug" Carlton Mellick III - Using clones of the Baby Jesus for anal sex will be the hip sex fetish of the future. **92 pages $10**

BB-008 "Fishyfleshed" Carlton Mellick III - The world of the past is an illogical flatland lacking in dimension and color, a sick-scape of crispy squid people wandering the desert for no apparent reason. **260 pages $14**

BB-009 "Dead Bitch Army" Andre Duza - Step into a world filled with racist teenagers, cannibals, 100 warped Uncle Sams, automobiles with razor-sharp teeth, living graffiti, and a pissed-off zombie bitch out for revenge. **344 pages $16**

BB-010 "The Menstruating Mall" Carlton Mellick III *"The Breakfast Club* meets *Chopping Mall* as directed by David Lynch."* - Brian Keene **212 pages $12**

BB-011 "Angel Dust Apocalypse" Jeremy Robert Johnson - Meth-heads, man-made monsters, and murderous Neo-Nazis. "Seriously amazing short stories..." - Chuck Palahniuk, author of *Fight Club* **184 pages $11**

BB-012 "Ocean of Lard" Kevin L Donihe / Carlton Mellick III - A parody of those old Choose Your Own Adventure kid's books about some very odd pirates sailing on a sea made of animal fat. **176 pages $12**

   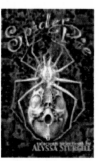

BB-013 "Last Burn in Hell" John Edward Lawson - From his lurid angst-affair with a lesbian music diva to his ascendance as unlikely pop icon the one constant for Kenrick Brimley, official state prison gigolo, is he's got no clue what he's doing. **172 pages $14**

BB-014 "Tangerinephant" Kevin Dole 2 - TV-obsessed aliens have abducted Michael Tangerinephant in this bizarre combination of science fiction, satire, and surrealism. **164 pages $11**

BB-015 "Foop!" Chris Genoa - Strange happenings are going on at Dactyl, Inc, the world's first and only time travel tourism company.
"A surreal pie in the face!" - Christopher Moore **300 pages $14**

BB-016 "Spider Pie" Alyssa Sturgill - A one-way trip down a rabbit hole inhabited by sexual deviants and friendly monsters, fairytale beginnings and hideous endings. **104 pages $11**

BB-017 "The Unauthorized Woman" Efrem Emerson - Enter the world of the inner freak, a landscape populated by the pre-dead and morticioners, by cockroaches and 300-lb robots. **104 pages $11**

BB-018 "Fugue XXIX" Forrest Aguirre - Tales from the fringe of speculative literary fiction where innovative minds dream up the future's uncharted territories while mining forgotten treasures of the past. **220 pages $16**

BB-019 "Pocket Full of Loose Razorblades" John Edward Lawson - A collection of dark bizarro stories. From a giant rectum to a foot-fungus factory to a girl with a biforked tongue. **190 pages $13**

BB-020 "Punk Land" Carlton Mellick III - In the punk version of Heaven, the anarchist utopia is threatened by corporate fascism and only Goblin, Mortician's sperm, and a blue-mohawked female assassin named Shark Girl can stop them. **284 pages $15**

BB-021 "Pseudo-City" D. Harlan Wilson - Pseudo-City exposes what waits in the bathroom stall, under the manhole cover and in the corporate boardroom, all in a way that can only be described as mind-bogglingly irreal. **220 pages $16**

BB-022 "Kafka's Uncle and Other Strange Tales" Bruce Taylor - Anslenot and his giant tarantula (tormentor? fri-end?) wander a desecrated world in this novel and collection of stories from Mr. Magic Realism Himself. **348 pages $17**

BB-023 "Sex and Death In Television Town" Carlton Mellick III - In the old west, a gang of hermaphrodite gunslingers take refuge from a demon plague in Telos: a town where its citizens have televisions instead of heads. **184 pages $12**

BB-024 "It Came From Below The Belt" Bradley Sands - What can Grover Goldstein do when his severed, sentient penis forces him to return to high school and help it win the presidential election? **204 pages $13**

BB-025 "Sick: An Anthology of Illness" John Lawson, editor - These Sick stories are horrendous and hilarious dissections of creative minds on the scalpel's edge. **296 pages $16**

BB-026 "Tempting Disaster" John Lawson, editor - A shocking and alluring anthology from the fringe that examines our culture's obsession with taboos. **260 pages $16**

BB-027 "Siren Promised" Jeremy Robert Johnson - Nominated for the Bram Stoker Award. A potent mix of bad drugs, bad dreams, brutal bad guys, and surreal/incredible art by Alan M. Clark. **190 pages $13**

BB-028 "Chemical Gardens" Gina Ranalli - Ro and punk band *Green is the Enemy* find Kreepkins, a surfer-dude warlock, a vengeful demon, and a Metal Priestess in their way as they try to escape an underground nightmare. **188 pages $13**

BB-029 "Jesus Freaks" Andre Duza For God so loved the world that he gave his only two begotten sons... and a few million zombies. **400 pages $16**

BB-030 "Grape City" Kevin L. Donihe - More Donihe-style comedic bizarro about a demon named Charles who is forced to work a minimum wage job on Earth after Hell goes out of business. **108 pages $10**

BB-031"Sea of the Patchwork Cats" Carlton Mellick III - A quiet dreamlike tale set in the ashes of the human race. For Mellick enthusiasts who also adore *The Twilight Zone*. **112 pages $10**

BB-032 "Extinction Journals" Jeremy Robert Johnson - An uncanny voyage across a newly nuclear America where one man must confront the problems associated with loneliness, insane dieties, radiation, love, and an ever-evolving cockroach suit with a mind of its own. **104 pages $10**

BB-033 **"Meat Puppet Cabaret"** Steve Beard At last! The secret connection between Jack the Ripper and Princess Diana's death revealed! **240 pages $16 / $30**

BB-034 **"The Greatest Fucking Moment in Sports"** Kevin L. Donihe - In the tradition of the surreal anti-sitcom *Get A Life* comes a tale of triumph and agape love from the master of comedic bizarro. **108 pages $10**

BB-035 **"The Troublesome Amputee"** John Edward Lawson - Disturbing verse from a man who truly believes nothing is sacred and intends to prove it. **104 pages $9**

BB-036 **"Deity"** Vic Mudd God (who doesn't like to be called "God") comes down to a typical, suburban, Ohio family for a little vacation—but it doesn't turn out to be as relaxing as He had hoped it would be... **168 pages $12**

BB-037 **"The Haunted Vagina"** Carlton Mellick III - It's difficult to love a woman whose vagina is a gateway to the world of the dead. **132 pages $10**

BB-038 **"Tales from the Vinegar Wasteland"** Ray Fracalossy - Witness: a man is slowly losing his face, a neighbor who periodically screams out for no apparent reason, and a house with a room that doesn't actually exist. **240 pages $14**

BB-039 **"Suicide Girls in the Afterlife"** Gina Ranalli - After Pogue commits suicide, she unexpectedly finds herself an unwilling "guest" at a hotel in the Afterlife, where she meets a group of bizarre characters, including a goth Satan, a hippie Jesus, and an alien-human hybrid. **100 pages $9**

BB-040 **"And Your Point Is?"** Steve Aylett - In this follow-up to LINT multiple authors provide critical commentary and essays about Jeff Lint's mind-bending literature. **104 pages $11**

BB-041 "Not Quite One of the Boys" Vincent Sakowski -While drug-dealer Maxi drinks with Dante in purgatory, God and Satan play a little tri-level chess and do a little bargaining over his business partner, Vinnie, who is still left on earth. **220 pages $14**

BB-042 "Teeth and Tongue Landscape" Carlton Mellick III - On a planet made out of meat, a socially-obsessive monophobic man tries to find his place amongst the strange creatures and communities that he comes across. **110   pages $10**

BB-043 "War Slut" Carlton Mellick III - Part "1984," part "Waiting for Godot," and part action horror video game adaptation of John Carpenter's "The Thing." **116 pages $10**

BB-044 "All Encompassing Trip" Nicole Del Sesto -In a world where coffee is no longer available, the only television shows are reality TV re-runs, and the animals are talking back, Nikki, Amber and a singing Coyote in a do-rag are out to restore the light **308 pages $15**

BB-045 "Dr. Identity" D. Harlan Wilson - Follow the Dystopian Duo on a killing spree of epic proportions through the irreal postcapitalist city of Bliptown where time ticks sideways, artificial Bug-Eyed Monsters punish citizens for consumer-capitalist lethargy, and ultraviolence is as essential as a daily multivitamin. **208 pages $15**

BB-046 "The Million-Year Centipede" Eckhard Gerdes -Wakelin, frontman for 'The Hinge,' wrote a poem so prophetic that to ignore it dooms a person to drown in blood. **130 pages $12**

BB-047 "Sausagey Santa" Carlton Mellick III - A bizarro Christmas tale featuring Santa as a piratey mutant with a body made of sausages. **124 pages $10**

BB-048 "Misadventures in a Thumbnail Universe" Vincent Sakowski - Dive deep into the surreal and satirical realms of neo-classical Blender Fiction, filled with television shoes and flesh-filled skies. **120 pages $10**

BB-049 "Vacation" Jeremy C. Shipp - Blueblood Bernard Johnson leaved his boring life behind to go on The Vacation, a year-long corporate sponsored odyssey. But instead of seeing the world, Bernard is captured by terrorists, becomes a key figure in secret drug wars, and, worse, doesn't once miss his secure American Dream. **160 pages $14**

BB-050 "Discouraging at Best" John Edward Lawson - A collection where the absurdity of the mundane expands exponentially creating a tidal wave that sweeps reason away. For those who enjoy satire, bizarro, or a good old-fashioned slap to the senses. **208 pages $15**

BB-051 "13 Thorns" Gina Ranalli - Thirteen tales of twisted, bizarro horror. **240 pages $13**

BB-052 "Better Ways of Being Dead" Christian TeBordo - In this class, the students have to keep one palm down on the table at all times, and listen to lectures about a panda who speaks Chinese. **216 pages $14**

BB-053 "Ballad of a Slow Poisoner" Andrew Goldfarb Millford Mutterwurst sat down on a Tuesday to take his afternoon tea, and made the unpleasant discovery that his elbows were becoming flatter. **128 pages $10**

BB-054 "Wall of Kiss" Gina Ranalli A woman... A wall... Sometimes love blooms in the strangest of places. **108 pages $9**

BB-055 "HELP! A Bear is Eating Me" Mykle Hansen The bizarro, heartwarming, magical tale of poor planning, hubris and severe blood loss... **150 pages $11**

BB-056 "Piecemeal June" Jordan Krall A man falls in love with a living sex doll, but with love comes danger when her creator comes after her with crab-squid assassins. **90 pages $9**

BB-057 **"Laredo"** **Tony Rauch** Dreamlike, surreal stories by Tony Rauch. **180 pages** **$12**

BB-058 **"The Overwhelming Urge"** **Andersen Prunty** A collection of bizarro tales by Andersen Prunty. **150 pages** **$11**

BB-059 **"Adolf in Wonderland"** **Carlton Mellick III** A dreamlike adventure that takes a young descendant of Adolf Hitler's design and sends him down the rabbit hole into a world of imperfection and disorder. **180 pages** **$11**

BB-060 **"Super Cell Anemia"** **Duncan B. Barlow** "Unrelentingly bizarre and mysterious, unsettling in all the right ways..." - Brian Evenson. **180 pages** **$12**

BB-061 **"Ultra Fuckers"** **Carlton Mellick III** Absurdist suburban horror about a couple who enter an upper middle class gated community but can't find their way out. **108 pages** **$9**

BB-062 **"House of Houses"** **Kevin L. Donihe** An odd man wants to marry his house. Unfortunately, all of the houses in the world collapse at the same time in the Great House Holocaust. Now he must travel to House Heaven to find his departed fiancee. **172 pages** **$11**

BB-063 **"Necro Sex Machine"** **Andre Duza** **400 pages** he The Dead Bicth returns in this follow-up to the bizarro zombie epic Dead Bitch Army. **$16**

BB-063 **"Squid Pulp Blues"** **Jordan Krall** **204 pages** In these three bizarro-noir novellas, the reader is thrown into a world of murderers, drugs made from squid parts, deformed gun-toting veterans, and a mischievous apocalyptic donkey. **$13**

COMING SOON

"Cocoon of Terror" by Jason Earls
"Jack and Mr. Grin" by Andersen Prunty
"Macho Poni" by Lotus Rose
"Zerostrata" by Andersen Prunty
"Shark Hunting in Paradise Garden" by Cameron Pierce
"The Rampaging Fuckers of Everything on the Shitting
Planet of the Vomit Atmosphere" by Mykle Hansen
"Apeshit" by Carlton Mellick III

ORDER FORM

TITLES	QTY	PRICE	TOTAL

Please make checks and moneyorders payable to ROSE O'KEEFE / BIZARRO BOOKS in U.S. funds only. Please don't send bad checks! Allow 2-6 weeks for delivery. International orders may take longer. If you'd like to pay online via PAYPAL.COM, send payments to publisher@eraserheadpress.com.

SHIPPING: US ORDERS - $2 for the first book, $1 for each additional book. For priority shipping, add an additional $4. INT'L ORDERS - $5 for the first book, $3 for each additional book. Add an additional $5 per book for global priority shipping.

Send payment to:

BIZARRO BOOKS
 C/O Rose O'Keefe
 205 NE Bryant
 Portland, OR 97211

Address

City   State   Zip

Email   Phone

Breinigsville, PA USA
12 October 2009
225593BV00001B/21/P